BANTAM

T0158755

BANTAM

A Novella

MASON JOINER

iUniverse, Inc.
Bloomington

Bantam

Copyright © 2011 by Mason Joiner

All rights reserved. No part of this book may be used or reproduced by any means, graphic, electronic, or mechanical, including photocopying, recording, taping or by any information storage retrieval system without the written permission of the publisher except in the case of brief quotations embodied in critical articles and reviews.

This is a work of fiction. All of the characters, names, incidents, organizations, and dialogue in this novel are either the products of the author's imagination or are used fictitiously.

iUniverse books may be ordered through booksellers or by contacting:

iUniverse
1663 Liberty Drive
Bloomington, IN 47403
www.iuniverse.com
1-800-Authors (1-800-288-4677)

Because of the dynamic nature of the Internet, any web addresses or links contained in this book may have changed since publication and may no longer be valid. The views expressed in this work are solely those of the author and do not necessarily reflect the views of the publisher, and the publisher hereby disclaims any responsibility for them.

Any people depicted in stock imagery provided by Thinkstock are models, and such images are being used for illustrative purposes only.
Certain stock imagery © Thinkstock.

ISBN: 978-1-4620-4301-9 (sc)
ISBN: 978-1-4620-4302-6 (ebk)

Printed in the United States of America

iUniverse rev. date: 07/30/2011

Acknowledgments

The making of *Bantam* was most certainly not a one-man show. I cannot morally send this story out to the world without first recognizing all the hands that guided me along the way. While there are many names even beyond this list, the following are the major players who helped me throughout the process of penning this book. First and foremost, I would like to thank Dr. Clayton Delery for leading me through the process of writing *Bantam.* His frank and constructive feedback proved quite invaluable. Next, Dr. Nahla Beier and Dr. Benjamin Lasseter for taking the time from their busy teaching schedules to read my work and supply useful criticism; Dr. Robert Dalling for his practical publication advice; my parents, Mike and Melinda Joiner, who always provide ample love and support; my wonderful sister, Micah Joiner, who was with me through every step of revision; and finally, Misha Molani, my first peer reader. Many thanks to all of the names above, as well as the countless unmentioned. *Bantam* would be an entirely different creature without your extraordinary aid.

Late 1960's

They drove by in streaks of white, black, red and silver. Streetlights reflected off their chrome hubcaps and tailfins. Oramus' unwashed hands gripped the night air like a steering wheel. From his vantage point on the roof of the abandoned Motor City Inn, Oramus watched the cars wind through the familiar grid system. A giant advertisement was plastered across the building opposite him: *LBJ for the USA. The stakes are too high for you to stay at home.* Oramus' older brother, Lex, seized his right hand and tugged, separating reluctant Oramus from his peaceful view. Lex guided Oramus up the sloping roof to its crest where he lifted a trap door and allowed Oramus to descend a wooden ladder. Lex followed his brother down the ladder and closed the hatch above him, immersing the boys in pitch-blackness. Lex's feet slapped the floor. The boys entered a stuffy stairwell and started down the flights. The concrete steps were gritty beneath their bare toes. Breathing the stale air quietly, so as not to wake the hotel's non-existent tenants, they tiptoed down seven flights of stairs. Oramus shoved open a heavy door leading into a cool, tiled room. A lantern surrounded by three burlap potato sacks sat on the floor near the opposite wall. A steadily breathing figure filled one sack. Lex and Oramus crossed the spacious room, glanced a goodnight to one another and slithered into their bedrolls.

~

A clatter rang in the lobby of the old Motor City Inn, jarring the two young boys from their sleep. One mumbled as he leaned on an elbow, searching the room with half-open eyes the color of fresh grass. The other lay on his back, white arms folded over his face.

"Time to wake up, boys. I'm opening the shop soon," said a deep and welcoming voice. Ellis Dyce puffed slightly as he bent over to recover the wrench he had dropped. He placed the tool in a pocket of the oily coveralls that always clothed his husky body. Ellis walked behind the lobby reception desk where he manned his used hardware kiosk. His leather brogans clopped across the tile floor.

The boys folded their pallets, stacked them in a corner and brushed dirt off their tattered clothes. The younger boy grabbed the green kerosene lantern, bringing it to a shelf behind the desk. "Dad, can me and Lex play outside today?" he asked. The green-eyed boy had already begun scooting toward the back door.

"Oramus, you know I need your help around the shop." Oramus clasped Ellis' pant-leg and smiled. Ellis heaved a lengthy sigh and said, "But I suppose you can."

Lex cheered. "Thanks, Dad!"

Ellis lightly messed Oramus' brown curls with his thick fingers. "You're welcome. Just be careful! You know how dangerous it is out in the alleys."

"We'll be careful, Dad," Lex spurted.

"Hold on," his father continued. "Come over here, Lex. I'm going to pray over you." Ellis laid a hand on each of his sons' backs and pressed them to his body. "Lord, protect them and keep them and send angels to watch over them today. In Jesus' name we pray. And what do we say, boys?"

"Amen," the brothers said in unison.

"Amen. Now go have fun."

The boys broke away from their father's hold and dashed to the back door. Lex made it out first.

Oramus was almost through the door when Ellis shouted, "Wait! I'm sorry, Oramus. There's one thing I need you to do before you go."

Oramus stopped himself at the doorframe and slowly turned to meet Ellis' beseeching gaze.

"I promise this won't take long. You can catch up with Lex in a minute. There are some washers caught under that refrigerator. Do you mind reaching under there and fishing them out for me?"

Oramus scampered behind the reception desk to complete the chore.

Outside, Lex straightened the sign hanging on their door. It was a piece of cardboard with *Hardware Store* scrawled in paint. Glancing right at a busy roadway, he zipped left down the alley to a tall, wooden fence. Without hesitating, he crawled through a hole at the base. He could now see the red awning; Lex ran as fast as his legs would move.

The doorbell buzzed at his touch. Behind the black, iron screen, a rich brown door opened, revealing the landlady. She raised a finely plucked eyebrow over a pair of horn-rimmed glasses and growled through thin, red lips, "The Leers?"

"Mhm."

The landlady abruptly shut the door, and Lex stood frozen for several seconds. Finally, she re-emerged from her lair. "Okay. You can come in." She pulled a set of keys from her belt and pinched one with long, bony talons. She twisted the key and thrust the screen open, allowing Lex to pass. He shakily stepped into the apartment building lit only by sconces on either side of the door and horizontal rungs of sunlight peering through a Venetian blind. Appropriate atmosphere for an undercover dragon. The foyer smelled of cigarette smoke and chocolate chip cookies. Lex crept toward the staircase as the landlady locked the screen behind him. The rough stairs creaked under Lex's weight. The further he climbed away from the landlady, the spunkier his steps became. When he reached the second floor, Lex ambled down the hall to the last apartment. He timidly knocked on the door and looked up, smiling at the peephole. He heard a woman's muffled call from inside.

"Ivess! Lex is here!"

A masculine voice followed. "Tell him to go away. She's about to have breakfast!"

"Please, dear, he can probably hear you," the mature female voice countered.

"I don't care. I don't want my daughter hanging around some filthy street kid!"

"Hush, Claude!"

The dull doorknob turned, and a small girl slipped into the hall with an apologetic expression. She immediately embraced Lex. Taken aback, he was slow to return the hug. He inhaled the lavender scent of her waist-length, wavy, brown hair.

"Hi, Lex," she whispered.

"Hi," the boy stuttered.

Ivess pried herself away with a wide, shining smile.

Scrambling for conversation, Lex spouted, "Is that a new dress?"

Ivess examined her purple sundress splotched with white polka dots and playfully swished the skirt. "Not really. It was my Easter dress last year."

"Oh."

"But I never wore it again until this summer."

Lex observed his own appearance: blackish, unshod feet; shaggy, black hair; stained, cotton shorts; and a ripped, once-white shirt. He blushed.

Ivess giggled. "It's all right, Lex. I like you."

Lex's eyes rose to meet hers, and a smile grew. Ivess pulled his hand from his pocket and laced their fingers together. Lex swallowed. She grinned and led him to a window at the end of the hall. Lex admired the girl's pale blue eyes. Their heads drew cautiously near. The distance between their faces seemed a football field. Frequently hesitating, their heads moved in spurts until they were close enough to feel each other's breath on their lips.

Tap!

The pair jumped, bumping foreheads.

Tap!

Lex glared out the window.

Tap!

Oramus was on the ground, throwing pebbles at them. Lex squinted, staring furiously at his brother. Oramus laughed hysterically. Lex spun at the sound of an opening door.

"Ivess, your breakfast is getting cold," said her father, a man in dark brown slacks and a tucked-in, white button-down.

"Coming, Daddy," Ivess replied, shuffling toward her father.

"I guess I'll see you 'round," Lex suggested.

Her father scowled.

"I guess. Bye, Lex." She showed that same apologetic expression as before.

Lex lifted a somber hand to wave as Mr. Leer prompted his daughter inside. "Bye." He was cut off by the sharp click of the door closing. He gazed at where Ivess had been standing until he remembered his brother's prank. A smirk came to Lex's chapped lips as he zipped down the hall. He took the stairs two-by-two, until the glare of the fire-haired landlady sucking on a cigarette in the doorway congealed his muscles. She opened the front door and unbolted the screen. Lex whizzed out and raced down the alley before she could scorch his rump. Oramus bounded only a few yards ahead.

"You're going to pay for that, you little twerp!"

Oramus responded with kissing noises.

The pursuit began. Lex and Oramus sprinted to the fence. At the last moment, Oramus leapt sideways and led his brother up a fire escape. From the second level, they slid down the ladder onto the other side of the fence. Oramus took flight down the alley, Lex at his tail. He squeezed between two trashcans, pushing one into his brother's path; Lex hurdled the obstacle with ease.

When the brothers turned the nearest corner, they found themselves wading through a strong current of Detroit residents making their way to work. Voices, car horns and bicycle bells bombarded the boys' eardrums. The smells of coffee, perfume, cigarette-smoke and exhaust blended into a stuffy, urban reek. Lex and Oramus kept their heads low, observing a variety of footwear pound the sidewalk. Their lack of shoes made it difficult to avoid getting their toes mashed.

The boys were finally able to squeeze out of the herd and continue their chase down the next alley. Lex was steadily falling behind, and Oramus was determined to lose him. He dove around the next corner he reached. Inertia propelled Lex forward. Before Oramus could recover, he torpedoed into a man's back. The impact knocked Oramus to the ground. The man turned menacingly, a furious eye hunting for the culprit. His other eye socket was patched. The man spotted Oramus, who lay stunned at his feet.

"It's a damned ankle-biter! Where's my slugger?"

He clutched a baseball bat that was leaning against the adjacent brick building. Another man of skinnier, sicklier stature appeared from behind him.

"He's just a kid, man. Be cool."

The one-eyed brute gripped his counterpart securely under the jawbone, forcing blood to fill his gaunt features. "Back off, addict," the bully threatened. He tossed the puny man back and threw a small bag of orange pills at his chest. "Here's your sunshine." Next, the dealer shifted his attention to Oramus. He brandished the baseball bat, gripped it with both fists and prepared to swing.

Suddenly, Oramus felt two hands grasp his shoulders and pull. He heard the bat whoosh as he was hauled backward and heaved to his feet. Realizing that the savior's hands belonged to Lex, Oramus regained his wits and sprinted toward the bustling street with his brother.

The one-eyed man wiped his palm over a well-lacquered mane, dropped the bat and jogged after them. Fringe on the sleeves of his buckskin jacket fluttered behind.

The bully busted through the congestion of pedestrians and marched onto the road amid the morning traffic, trying not to lose sight of his prey. A car braked at his rear and sounded its earsplitting horn. He gave the grill a good kick with his new cowboy boot. Lex and Oramus were too far gone for the man to catch up. He scoured the area and spied an Oriental beanpole of a man sitting on the sidewalk, playing a guqin for spare change. The bully strode over and lifted him by the collar. The Oriental's guqin banged the cement with a reverberating thud. The bully slammed the scrawny guqin player onto the hood of a parallel-parked, yellow vehicle.

"Hey, gook," he mocked. "You got giant balls living in this country. I might decide to cut you straight down the middle right now. But I'm not going to. The way I see it, if you want to stay alive, you'll help me. You're a bum, aren't you? You know those two boys that just went by here?"

The guqin player gagged an answer to the best of his ability. "I—yes."

"Good for you. Where do they live?"

The guqin player shuddered and peeped, "Where?" His eyes cowered beneath trembling eyelids. Again, the bully bashed the Oriental's head on the hood of the lemony car. "I don't know! I don't know!" the Oriental whined.

"I think you do know. All you bums suck out of the same watering hole." The bully bashed him a third time.

"Okay, okay. There is old hotel over there," he jabbered, pointing a shaky, bent finger down the block. "Motor City Inn. But it's closed. Chains on the door! You must go 'round. Back door says 'hardware.' Worst building on the block."

The bully let go of the feeble man and patted his cheek. "Thanks, gook. You get to keep your throat today." He crushed the guqin under his boot and set a brisk pace for the hotel.

~

Lex and Oramus didn't stop running until they reached the railroad tracks a couple of miles away from the Motor

City Inn. Situated neatly between the fire station and a tall chain-link fence, the tracks seemed like a safe place to stop.

"Do you think he's still chasing us?" Oramus asked, gasping.

Lex shrugged. "I don't know." The brothers hurried across the railroad tracks. Exhausted, they plopped down with their backs against the fence. Oramus plucked blades of grass and dug in the dirt to pass time. Lex was thinking. "We'll run in there if he shows up," the boy said, pointing to the fire station.

As if answering his suggestion, the station erupted in shouts, and the fire truck rattled out of slumber. The long, red engine charged into the lonely street, sirens blazing. The boys watched, mesmerized, until the horn vacated their ears entirely.

"Do you think we can go now?" Oramus proposed.

"No. Let's wait a little while."

~

The lobby door swung open with a rusty squeal. A tall man sauntered in, arms folded. Ellis stood up from his workbench behind the counter and smeared his greasy hands on his jumpsuit. He thought the customer looked like trouble, as he had an eye-patch and a biker jacket.

"Hullo, hullo. Can I help you?" He came out from behind the desk to shake his visitor's hand. The man rejected his advance.

"Do you have a commercial license to run this place?"

Ellis chuckled uncomfortably. "Not officially. But I've been selling hardware here for over a year without any trouble. Why do you ask?"

"Just curious."

"So what is your business here, then?"

"I need a hammer."

"Oh. Well then," Ellis sighed. Returning behind the desk, he inquired, "What kind? I got claw, ball-peen, beetle, lump, sledge, stonemasons, mauls, mallets . . ."

"Which is the best quality?"

Ellis chose a hammer from his inventory rack and brought it to the customer. "Well, for nailing, this claw hammer's about the sturdiest you can find. Solid steel head."

The customer took the hammer and hefted it. "This'll do."

"Alrighty. Seventy cents."

The customer reached into his jean pocket and pulled out a few coins. He pressed two quarters and two dimes into Ellis' open palm. The store owner clenched the sum in a dense fist and retrieved a shoebox labeled *revenue* from under the counter.

"D'you lose that eye in the war?" asked Ellis.

"That depends. There's a lot of wars out there, Mister. Some you don't even know about."

Shaking his head, Ellis replied, "Anyway, thank you for stopping by. Hope the hammer treats you well. Is there anything else I can do for you?"

"Well, now that you mention it, I'm curious. Don't you think you'd get more business out on the street instead of holed up in this dump?"

"I have a good deal in my inventory. I figure this is the best way to keep it all under shelter, don't you? Besides, I've run this place for eighteen months. Most people who need hardware around here know where to find me."

The customer licked his lips. "Two kids; about ten; grubby. You know them?"

"My boys?"

The man grimly smiled, showing a set of yellowed teeth. Wordless, he started for the exit.

"Who are you? Why did you ask about my children?" Ellis demanded. "Is something wrong? Has something happened to them?" Ellis rushed after the man and grabbed his shoulder. "Speak!"

The stranger whirled around and knocked Ellis on all fours. A razor-sharp pang throbbed in his mouth, which flooded with warm liquid. He spewed the reservoir and a collection of teeth and licked the newfound chasm in his gums to excruciating nerve spasms. A boot stepped into view. Ellis looked up just in time to glimpse the falling hammer-head.

~

As the boys neared home, sirens urged them to move faster. A corner peeled back to show red, blue and orange lights flashing wildly. The street around the hotel was barricaded. Lex and Oramus made for the alley across the road, which seemed to be the hub of commotion. A troupe of firemen left the building with their equipment, making room for a team in DPD jackets. A pair of patrol officers took post behind them, blockading the entrance.

One of the guards spotted Lex and Oramus staggering toward the doorway. He swiftly paced up to them, shouting, "Whoa, whoa, whoa! What are you two doing here?"

The boys stared dumbly.

"You need to go home."

"We live here," Lex answered.

"You live here?"

The boy nodded.

"Um—" the officer stalled. "Okay, just wait right here. Don't move." He jogged to his squad car.

Shortly, four men exited the hotel lobby carrying a long, black bag. Lex and Oramus watched the procession, immobile.

"Let's get out of here," Lex whispered. He clutched his brother's arm. They slipped out under the lofty fence to avoid notice on the street.

When the boys reached sidewalk again, they ran blocks away from the scene, finally resting at a bus stop and newspaper stand. Oramus sank to his haunches, back against a wall.

Timidly, he asked, "Lex, was Dad in that bag?"

Lex eyed the concrete. At length, he replied faintly, "Yeah."

Oramus' lips tightened; his brow constricted. Feigning anger, he glared from left to right.

The brothers' eyes were wreathed in pink.

Tears kept them wordless for a lasting spell. Oramus swallowed. "So where are we going to go?"

"I don't know."

A hefty stack of the *Detroit Free Press* captured Lex's interest. He touched the top copy, focusing on the central photograph.

"How about this place? Let's go here," Lex said. He showed the paper to Oramus who stood and observed the picture. It depicted a colossal rocket hauled by a square tow-truck. White buildings and palm trees surrounded the convoy.

"Where's that?" questioned Oramus.

"I don't know. I bet someone will, though."

"How are we going to get there?"

Lex thought for a moment. "We'll walk." He rolled up the newspaper and shoved it into his pocket.

"Excuse me!" Only then were the boys aware of a white-haired newspaper salesman sitting on the other side of the stand. "The *Free Press* costs ten cents."

"I don't have any money."

"Then you can't have the paper!"

"I'll take it," said a new voice. A man wearing a brown suit and carrying a large suitcase came from behind Lex and slapped a dime onto the stand. Turning his back on the sneering merchant, the stranger showed himself to be the spectacled guqin player. "Hello." He gestured toward the bus stop. Lex and Oramus obeyed in shock of his transformed appearance. His pointed jaw was clean-shaven, and his stringy, black hair was combed over and pomaded.

The boys sat on either side of a bench, leaving room in the middle for the guqin player, who laid the voluminous suitcase flat on his lap and laced his fingers on top.

"Well, isn't this a surprise?"

"You're the guy who plays that funny guitar on our block," Oramus remarked.

"Yes, I am. I'm glad you remember."

Oramus felt the fabric of Fao-cun's jacket. "How—"

"Oh yes. I bet this is a bit confusing. To begin, my name is Dr. Fao-cun Bonfois. I am a teacher at the University of Lambshire near London. Lex, is it? Short for Alexander, I presume. And you, your name is Oramus. How do you do?" He offered a hand slanted downward to Oramus, who shook it, and then to Lex, who declined.

"How'd you know our names? Have you been following us?" Lex interrogated.

"No, no. I'm here to catch a bus. And as for your names, well, I've sat on your block long enough to pick them up. Of course, I'm not actually a derelict, though. I'm here for research, studying the spirituality of poverty. That 'funny guitar' is called a guqin; it's an ancient Chinese instrument." Fao-cun continued with a grudging exhale. "But, alas, the university has called me back to teach this semester, so I must return." He adjusted his glasses. "I'm curious. What are you two doing here thieving newspapers?"

"We're leaving Detroit," Oramus stated.

"By yourselves?"

"Our Dad's dead," Lex clarified.

Fao-cun clenched his teeth, and Oramus' face crinkled once again.

Fao-cun placed a hand on the child's back. "I know, I know; death is not a pleasant thing—at first anyway. But you'll learn, as we all do, that it's necessary—even precious. In death, your father will finally get the honor and respect he deserves. He was a fine man."

"You never even knew him!" Lex fired.

"It's a shame that's true. Come; let's talk about something else. Why did you steal that paper?"

"Show him, Lex. Show him," Oramus prodded, tears drying.

Lex removed the paper from his shorts and allowed Fao-cun to spread it out on top of his suitcase.

"We want to go here," Lex declared, thumping the picture.

"Ah! Can you read?"

Lex's cheeks pinked. He shook his head.

"No, no, no, no, no. No worries. I can teach you. I can teach you both."

"Really?" Oramus chirped.

"Of course. We'll have our first lesson right now. Here. This reads"—Fao-cun began while underlining the headline of the newspaper with his index finger—"*Apollo 7 To Launch October.*"

"What's that?" asked Oramus.

"Apollo Seven?" Fao-cun hunched down to Oramus' level. "A spaceship!"

"Whoa!" the child roared. "It's a spaceship, Lex!"

"Okay, okay. We're learning to read, remember?" Fao-cun reminded.

"Yeah."

"This symbol," he began, pointing to a letter, "is called an 'A'. It makes an *ah* sound, like 'ask' or 'apple'. This one is a 'T' which makes a *tuh* sound, like 'token.' Now repeat that. What is the name of this one?"

"A," replied Oramus.

"How does it sound?"

"*Ah.*"

"And this one?"

"T."

"And how does it sound?"

"*Tuh.*"

"Good job." Fao-cun pulled a fat, blue pen from his coat pocket and drew a C in the top corner of the newspaper. "This is called a 'C'. It makes a *cuh* sound like 'cold.' You have that?"

"Yes," said Oramus.

"Then how would you spell the word, 'cat'?" Fao-cun pronounced each sound distinctly.

Oramus stared at the newspaper for some seconds.

"C. A. T?"

"Yes, Oramus! That's excellent!" Fao-cun cheered.

Oramus lit like the sun. "I got it right?"

"Absolutely."

"You do it, Lex!" shouted Oramus.

"No, I don't want to play." Lex glowered, shying from the adult's gaze.

"Are you sure, Lex?" Fao-cun queried.

Lex nodded. The distant surge of a booming engine revealed the bus trucking its way down the bricked street.

"I want to spell something else," said Oramus eagerly.

"I'm sorry. We can't now. The bus is almost here. I'll tell you what. Come with me to London."

Oramus was blank-faced.

"Think about it! You'll be going to grade school at one of the most prestigious colleges in the world!" Fao-cun laughed. "What do you say?"

"Really?"

"Really," Fao-cun affirmed in the most sincere tone Oramus had ever heard from a stranger.

Oramus looked to his brother, who wore a distrustful expression.

Fao-cun stood. "Come with me now. I'm taking this bus to the airport."

The bus halted alongside the curb, sighing. Oramus hopped off the bench to join his new friend. Looking back, he saw that his brother hadn't moved.

"Lex—"

"I'm not going," he stated defiantly.

Fao-cun extended a hand to the boy. "Alexander—"

"That's not my name."

"Lex!" Oramus pleaded.

"I said I'm not going! You can go if you want to! I don't care!" Lex screamed. He left the bench and flew away in the opposite direction. Oramus tried to lunge after him, but Fao-cun grabbed his wrist. The grown man kneeled and braced Oramus' shoulders.

"Oramus, we haven't the time to chase him right now. I have to take this flight. Are you positive that you want to come with me to London? If so, it would mean letting him go for the moment."

"I don't know."

"You would not hurt my feelings if you chose to stay with your brother. I would understand. But I will also say that this opportunity may never come again."

Oramus blinked back tears.

"I promise you this. When we get to London, I'll do everything in my power to find Lex and bring him to us."

The bus driver honked. "You staying, you going?"

"You have to choose now, Oramus."

Oramus gazed down the street but could no longer see his older brother. Why had he run away? This was the best thing that could have happened to them. Oramus didn't know what to do. Ellis had always told them to take any chance they could to get off the streets. Oramus shook off Fao-cun's hold and dashed up the stairs into the city bus. Fao-cun rose and lugged the cumbersome suitcase up the stairs behind the boy. He fished for change in his coat pocket and dropped the toll into a dish near the steering wheel.

Directing his gaze down the aisle, he spotted Oramus sitting on the fifth row with his sullen head propped against the window. Fao-cun wove his way down the aisle through a maze of knees and baggage. He crashed into the seat beside Oramus as the bus crept forward. The moan of its engine rose in pitch as the bus accelerated, dampening the incessant chatter of the overhead radio.

The interior of the bus was dingy. Fao-cun scratched hardened beverage and condiment stains on the seat and scraped his shoe over unidentifiable black blemishes on the floor. He stared at the man in front of him and watched tiny orbs of sweat dip between the rolls of fat on the back of his neck. Fao-cun inhaled a lung-full of body odor. It seemed to radiate from that single man's head.

Fao-cun restlessly tapped his knees like a piano. He asked Oramus, "Do you know where London is?"

At first, Oramus didn't respond. However, after a few seconds, he looked timidly at Fao-cun. "Where?"

Fao-cun's countenance burst into a grin. He hoisted the suitcase onto his lap, flicked loose its clasps and opened its jaws. Oramus was astonished to find that the shell was next to empty. A broad, bulky atlas lay beside a rectangular, wooden box and a single change of clothes. Fao-cun picked up the book and shuffled through the pages until he found the correct map. Once again retrieving the pen from his coat pocket, he circled a large area under a cluster of lakes on the North American continent.

"You do know how maps work, correct? Blue is water; green is land."

Oramus nodded.

"Good. This is where you live," said Fao-cun, pointing to the encircled chunk.

"All that is Detroit?"

"No, no, no." Fao-cun made a dot within the circle. "Detroit is about right there. But this entire area is—"

"Michigan?"

"Yes, that's right. Michigan. And across the Atlantic Ocean on this big island we call Great Britain is the City of London." Fao-cun made another dot. "That's where we're going." He closed the atlas. "You'll need a passport. Do you know what that is?"

Oramus shook his head.

"A passport is a little booklet that says you can get into Great Britain. You'll need to have one, or they won't let you in."

"But I don't have one!" the boy interjected.

"That's okay, it's okay," Fao-cun hushed. "A couple years back, a professor at the university, Dr. Esau Roma, went on a charity mission to Central Africa. He met a boy suffering from malaria—a disease spread by mosquitoes. The disease was still young, so Dr. Roma was determined to save the boy. He decided to take him back to England for professional medical help. The trouble was getting a passport. So, to make a long story short, Dr. Ames, the president of the college, pulled a few strings and managed to get the boy into England. Dr. Ames has a reputation for philanthropy—uh, charity." Fao-cun whispered the next part. "Ever since then, Dr. Ames provides all faculty traveling abroad with counterfeit passport kits." Fao-cun tapped the wooden box, flashing Oramus a wink.

Oramus looked pensive. "What is counter—?" He hesitated to try to finish the word.

"Counterfeit? I'm sorry; counterfeit means false." Fao-cun lowered his voice again. "We'll make you one when we get to the airport." He shut and relatched the suitcase.

Fao-cun quieted, leaving Oramus' ears vulnerable to the yammering radio. The astute, collected voice of a male news anchor droned, "This month, Judge Raynor Macabee will have served the U. S. District Court for the Eastern District of Michigan with a firm and just hand for thirty years. To celebrate this occasion, the Detroit City Council is honoring him with the James Witherell Achievement

Award. They will present the award to Judge Macabee on Friday at 2 p.m. outside the district courthouse on West Lafayette Boulevard. The public is encouraged to attend. Murder in the South Cass Corridor today. A man was clubbed to death in the deserted Motor City Inn. The body was then burned with a kerosene lantern. No news yet on the identity of the victim or any suspects. WWJ News will continue to update you, Detroit, as the situation unfolds."

As the anchor carried on, Oramus thought about Lex and whether he should have followed him. His brother's actions had seemed so rash, and taking the bus made more sense. However, the idea of never seeing his brother again began seeping into Oramus' mind. Lex was the only playmate Oramus ever had. They had spent nearly every day together for as long as Oramus could remember. He questioned the new friend sitting beside him. What about the man had drawn Oramus to trust him? Oramus had never encountered someone who so openly accepted him. He was not accustomed to such friendliness from strangers. Fao-cun treated him as an equal, as if he cared about the boy's well being, even as if he loved him. Oramus wondered what Lex saw in Fao-cun that he didn't like. Fao-cun did promise to find Lex once they reached London. Oramus assured himself that Fao-cun would succeed.

The boy's mind drifted to his father. Hearing that Ellis was permanently gone was like someone telling Oramus the sun would not rise tomorrow morning.

"Fao-cun."

"Yes, Oramus?"

"Do you know what happened to my Dad?"

Fao-cun's breath trembled. "Well, when you finally got away from that thug this morning, he gave up chasing you and went to the hotel. I'm sure you can guess the rest."

"How did he know where we live?"

For once, Fao-cun's response was not immediate. Meaningless filler escaped his open mouth. Finally, he answered, "I don't know. I guess he had seen you there before."

Oramus frowned, weighing the explanation in his head. "Why did he do it?"

"Not here, Oramus," Fao-cun shot. "We'll talk about it later."

Oramus woefully nodded as if he'd just been scolded. He resumed quietly staring out the window. Oramus heard Ellis often pray that an opportunity to receive an education would someday confront his sons. He figured that was ultimately why he was on a bus, traveling to an unknown destination with a man he hardly knew.

~

"We want you to look presentable. No need disturbing the fellow passengers," Fao-cun said. He dressed Oramus in a public bathroom of the Detroit Metro Airport. The boy felt a bit odd in Fao-cun's clunky loafers, tremendously rolled-up slacks and flannel button-down. Fao-cun made him wash his hands and face and held his curly mess of a head under the faucet. He combed the wet hair behind Oramus' ears. Next, Fao-cun gave Oramus a toothbrush and toothpaste that he had purchased in the airport. Oramus removed the cap from the tube and balled his fist, sending a stream of white toothpaste jetting into the sink. "No, no. Not too much! A gentle press will do!"

Oramus scraped a dab of paste onto the toothbrush. He brought the brush to his mouth and began to swing his arm in a gaping side-to-side motion.

"Try small circles," Fao-cun suggested. "Like so." He demonstrated with an invisible toothbrush.

Oramus mimicked his movements.

"Good. All along the fronts of your teeth. And don't forget the tops and backs."

Oramus recoiled his arm and smacked his lips together. "This feels funny," he complained.

"It must taste better." Fao-cun pushed back his jacket sleeve and gazed at his watch, lips pursed. "Two full minutes of teeth-brushing starting now."

Oramus stuck the toothbrush back into his mouth and continued brushing, while Fao-cun hummed metronomically.

As Fao-cun and Oramus exited the bathroom and headed toward their terminal, a clapping resounded from behind them. When they turned to face the noise, a man wearing a coat and fishing hat began to cheer. The man's eyelids were droopy, and he unsteadily shifted from leg to leg.

"That's right, gook, keep walking. Get the hell out of this country! Don't come back!"

A reserved woman, bundled in a light blanket, rushed to the man, clutched his arm and desperately pulled in the opposite direction. Her eyes painstakingly avoided Fao-cun.

"What's wrong, honey?" the man slurred. "Aren't you glad this gook is leaving the country? Maybe his friends will follow the gesture!" Fao-cun grabbed Oramus' shoulder and turned him away from the scene, setting a prudent pace for the terminal.

"Pay no attention to him, Oramus. He's drunk and ignorant."

"He called you a name. What did it mean?"

"Don't worry about it. In fact, take pride in not knowing. It's filthy."

~

London smelled mildewy. It had just rained, evidenced by water in the valleys between cobblestones that comprised the street. It was mid-morning; the flight had lasted all night. Fao-cun and Oramus spent most of the morning in the London airport waiting at baggage claim, nabbing a quick breakfast and explaining to the customs personnel why an Asian man in his thirties was tagging along a puny, Caucasian boy from America. After much artful convincing, Fao-cun was able to pass Oramus off as his adopted son, Oramus Bonfois.

Fao-cun was currently hailing a cab. Oramus stood a little ways behind. When Fao-cun finally reeled one in, he marched to the back, opened the trunk and wrestled his suitcase inside, waving away an offer of help from the driver. Shutting the lid, he returned to the side of the cab and opened the door for Oramus to get in. He swung his body into the cab and sealed it from the bustling outside commotion. Oramus wiggled his nose at the unappetizing mixture of cabbage and bitter herbal scents he didn't recognize.

"Lambshire University, please," Fao-cun said to the heavyset driver, who took a soft-bristle brush from the console to sweep back his thick, gray locks. The hair ended halfway down his neck. The driver looked over his shoulder, revealing a large, pear-like nose; everything south was stubble.

"Should be 'bout an hour drive." Oramus silently chortled when the driver spoke.

"Nasty rain lately?" Fao-cun inquired.

"Ain't seen sun in four days. Tuesd'y we got thirty centimeters. Paper says it should slack off by the weekend."

"That's good."

"Where you blokes from?"

"Well, I've lived in London for sixteen years. Just got back from a vacation in the United States. This is a friend of mine from Detroit."

"Pleased to meet you. Call me Ike."

"Dr. Fao-cun Bonfois. And this is Oramus."

"'Ullo. Doctor, eh? Physician?"

"No. Doctor of Theology."

"Ah. I been a cabby since I was a boy. Soon as I could drive, I was chauffeurin' people all over London. You blokes like stories?"

"I'm quite fond of a good story," said Fao-cun.

"Well 'ere goes. I'd been a cabby for about four years. 1924 I believe it were. An old geezer climbs in the back and says, 'Take me to the most out-o-the-way pub you know.' ''Ard day?' I ask. 'E says, 'Just go.' 'Alright,' says I, and I drives 'im to a pub on the other side o' town. Naturally, I tell 'im a story to pass the time, you know. When we got there he says, 'Wait 'ere.' So I gave the newspaper a bit of a shufty—catch up on news, you know. After a good 'our an' an 'alf, 'e comes weavin' out the pub back to me cab, and this time he says, 'Now take me to the opium den in Chinatown.' I say, 'Geez! You mus've 'ad a bloody terrible day!' 'Step on it,' 'e says to me. So I did. I brought 'im to the opium den in Chinatown, though I didn't much fancy going to Chinatown in those days. The chinks scared me a bit when I was a lad. No offense, Doc. I wait for another couple of 'ours jus' readin' me newspaper 'til 'e finally comes out again, wanderin' down the road. I 'onks for 'im and waves 'im over to me cab and 'e 'ops in the back. Once 'e flags where 'e is ('e's 'igh as a kite by now, you know), 'e says, 'Take me to the Brighton brothel, if you please.' So I turns to 'im, and you know what I says?" Approaching a traffic light, Ike slowed the vehicle to a halt and turned to face Oramus and Fao-cun. "I says, 'Well, Dad, I'll take you, but what does Mum 'ave to say 'bout it?'" The driver burst into laughter. Oramus must have missed the joke. He grinned politely anyway. Fao-cun chuckled, swallowing a grimace. "Don't worry, I'm full of 'em!"

Tuning out the boisterous cab driver, Oramus admired the English countryside. They were nearing the edge of town and the beginnings of verdant pastures became visible. Dark green hedges penciled a grid among the hills. Oramus spied a fat heifer resting in the shade of an elm. She was painted white and caramel and bore a satisfied look. Further down the road a crooked, brick well sat alone in a valley. Oramus glued his eyes to the well, unsure of its purpose but fascinated by its rather ancient look. Just before it left his line of sight, an apple-colored songbird lit on the rim. Oramus was so captivated by the hodgepodge of landmarks that he barely realized when the trip was over. They had driven into a town by way of a cottage-lined street. Ike drove into the heart of the village and stopped the car in front of an eminent building of topaz-colored stone. Behind an iron-gated archway, two pillars flowed from the ground up to a silver-plated awning. Avian statues perched at the apex. Snuggled between the pillars stood a stained cherry-wood door with cast iron hoops for handles. The entrance linked two close-set towers that peaked into needle-tipped roofs.

"'Ere we are. She's a pretty thing, ain't she? An absolute corker!" Ike exclaimed.

"Indeed," Fao-cun mumbled as he pushed open the car door and planted his feet outside.

"Easy goes it! Great chattin' with you."

"Yes, lovely," Fao-cun said. He closed the door and trudged to the trunk for his suitcase.

"Bye, Mr. Ike," Oramus cheeped.

"Bye now, lad." Ike slapped the boy's knee, and Oramus climbed out of the vehicle.

Fao-cun met him at the curb, dragging the suitcase at his heels. They stood side-by-side and waved Ike off. When he was far enough away, Fao-cun lowered his arm and looked at Oramus with wide, dark eyes.

"He was a talkative one!" Fao-cun wailed.

"I thought he was nice," rebutted Oramus.

"Well, no doubt, he had his charming moments—but devilishly crude ones as well. Not my sense of humor in the slightest." Fao-cun grinned. "And, besides, what would you know about it? Hardly paid attention at all! I don't think your eyes broke once from the other side of that window." Fao-cun turned to the iron gate. He dug around in his pocket and pulled out a ring of keys. Flipping through each one, he asked, "What were you staring at anyway?"

"The country. I like it. It's pretty here."

Fao-cun inhaled nostalgically. "Yes. You are very right about that, Oramus. Ah-ha!" he blurted, causing Oramus to jump. Fao-cun snatched up a copper key. "Here it is." He unlocked the gate. The iron purred as Fao-cun guided it open. He invited Oramus through the arch and re-latched the gate after the boy passed. They walked up a stone path lined with bushes blossoming white and gold and infusing the air with jasmine. The path led to a porch where Fao-cun and Oramus ascended three steps. Fao-cun tapped the knocker like a Morse key until he heard the turn of locking mechanisms on the other side. A pudgy woman emerged, fluffing her curly, orange hair. She let her glasses, which hung around her neck by a string of multicolored beads, bounce onto her white blouse.

"Dr. Bonfois! You're back! How was your trip, dear?"

"Fine, Allegra. Just fine. And how are you, my lovely?"

"Oh, working." The woman wiggled outside and enveloped Fao-cun in a motherly hug. Then she spun to face Oramus. "And who is this little man?"

"Allegra, this is Oramus. Oramus, this is Ms. Allegra, a secretary for the university. I met Oramus during my stay in America. He's actually going to be staying with me for a while."

"Very nice to meet you." She shook his hand daintily. "Dr. Bonfois, I want you to tell me all about your trip when you get the chance."

"I'd be glad to."

"Let's get you settled in! I'll tell Curtis to come get your luggage."

"Please. I'm sick of struggling with that wretched thing!"

Allegra re-mounted the glasses on her nose. She eagerly toddled back inside, calling "Curtis! Curtis!"

Oramus tugged Fao-cun's pant-leg.

"Hmm?"

"Who's Curtis?" he whispered.

"That's Ms. Allegra's son. She has him do odds and ends around the school. Follow me. We'll go see our room." They stepped over the threshold, encountering the pungent smell of ammonia, and onto a pearly, buffed tile floor. Oramus gaped at the enormous room. Directly in front of them was a vacant, enclosed booth where he guessed Ms. Allegra normally sat. On either side of the great hall, a green-carpeted staircase curved upward to a second story. At the top, they seemed to disappear behind the massive portrait of a chubby-cheeked man with eyes joyfully squinted. His upper lip was hidden under a silver walrus mustache. The man's hair was parted down the middle and cropped well above unusually large ears.

"Fao-cun, who's that?"

"Who?" Fao-cun queried, seeing no one around. "Oh, him!" he said, following Oramus' gaze. "That, Oramus, is the president of Lambshire University, Dr. Thurston Ames. He's been president since long before I arrived. You can tell from the picture he's a good-humored man. Unfortunately, he's rather senile these days. Surely he'll retire soon."

Oramus followed Fao-cun up the left staircase. Their shoes, which had loudly clapped against the tile, fell silent on the stairs' green carpet. As Oramus traveled up the staircase, his palm squeaked across a golden railing.

"Is this the college?" he asked Fao-cun.

"Part of it. The ground level holds all of the administrative offices. Housing for professors is on the second floor. The building where the actual learning takes place is behind this one, along with the boys' and girls' dormitories."

"I didn't know it would be so big."

"It's actually a tiny campus compared to most."

Fao-cun and Oramus turned behind the portrait, down a lengthy hallway full of doors. Halfway down the hall, Fao-cun stopped at a door marked *8*. He jammed a key into the wobbly doorknob. Fao-cun twisted the key over and over, each time with increasing vigor, before the door finally opened.

"Old locks," he griped. Oramus followed Fao-cun inside. "Well, here we are. Home sweet home. What do you think?"

Oramus' eyes danced across the room: the quaint, nookish kitchen with its honey-colored, wooden countertops, humming refrigerator and gleaming, unbroken appliances; the veteran couch ahead of him; a royal blue vase filled with brown, decrepit flowers centered atop a square dining table. "I like it."

Fao-cun chuckled quietly as Oramus absorbed the apartment. "Well, go on in. Have a seat. Get comfortable." Oramus removed his shoes. The sensation of carpet beneath his toes completed the strange ecstasy. Oramus pranced forward and sprang onto the couch.

Just as Fao-cun was closing the door, a voice slipped in. "Professor Bonfois."

Fao-cun rapidly poked his head back out into the hallway. He viewed a young, casually dressed man with shaggy, blonde hair. The visitor trudged toward him with his hard-shell suitcase.

"Hello, Curtis!" He flung the door open again. "Oh, drop that thing. I can get it from here. How was your summer?"

"Not bad, sir," the youth replied, releasing the suitcase.

Fao-cun embraced Curtis' hand with both of his own. "Your mother still has you working hard around here, I see."

"Yes, sir, as always."

"Well, you've grown your hair out. Gracious, boy! You look like the Wolfman! What happened to that clean-cut lad you were when I left?"

"I'm just trying it out, Dr. B."

"Oh really? And what does Allegra think of that?"

"What do you think?" the youth asked with a smirk.

"I think she thinks what I think. And I think it had better be cut before you step into my classroom this fall."

Curtis laughed helplessly. "Yes, sir."

"Well, I don't want to keep you from your chores."

"Yeah. I should get back to raking the courtyard." Curtis began strafing down the hall.

"Great seeing you, Curt."

"You too, Dr. B."

Fao-cun moved his suitcase inside, then shut and chained the door. "That's a good boy," he mumbled partly to Oramus and partly to himself. "Very respectful." Seizing the suitcase once more, Fao-cun charged into his bedroom and victoriously pitched the unwieldy object onto his bed. He returned into the living area with his hands on his hips. He looked at Oramus sprawled comfortably on the couch. "Let's finish getting you cleaned up."

~

Oramus splashed his bathwater, enjoying the distortion of his shadow on the floor of the porcelain bathtub. The bathroom was overbearingly white. The door, sink, toilet, tub and tile all gleamed the color of Michigan snow. The room even smelled white. Fao-cun had left the door cracked, so the two could communicate from separate rooms.

"How are you doing in there?" Fao-cun called from the dinner table.

"Fine," Oramus replied. His voice echoed in the small bathroom.

"Make sure to wash your hair well. I'm going to cut it when you get out, and I need it to be clean."

"Okay." Oramus leaned back and dipped his scalp in the water. Sitting up, he left a cloud of murk floating behind him.

"You know, Oramus, we've spent the last twenty-four hours together, yet we're still only acquaintances. I hardly know a thing about you. What's your middle name?"

"Marlon."

"Oramus Marlon Dyce."

"My real last name isn't Dyce."

"No?" Fao-cun squirmed in his chair.

"It's Krand. Dad isn't—wasn't my real father."

"He wasn't?"

"No. He adopted us. The agency told him my name, but they didn't know Lex's. Dad named him."

Fao-cun swiped his hair back upon his scalp. "So, obviously, you weren't always derelicts."

"No. Dad worked as a mechanic at a few places off-and-on for a long time. Just the last five or six years, we haven't had a real apartment or anything. We started living in the hotel a couple of years ago. Dad decided to sell tools and stuff, so we could buy food and maybe an apartment someday. He said we were going to be entrep . . ." Oramus struggled to mimic the word.

"Entrepreneurs." Fao-cun aided. "Why couldn't your father keep a job? He must have been a knowledgeable mechanic."

"Yeah. He was. He said he kept getting fired because he loved men instead of women."

"Oh. I see," Fao-cun paused timidly. "Well, what are your interests? What do you like?"

Oramus tapped the bathwater. "I don't know. Anything, I guess."

"Oh, come on. I'm sure you can think of something. Name one thing you're interested in."

"I like cars."

Fao-cun chuckled. "Cars. Yes, there's a typical American boy for you. Why do you like them?"

"I just like them, that's all," he answered bashfully, still drumming the water's surface.

"Don't clam up. Nothing to be ashamed of. Tell me about your dream car."

Oramus answered like a shot. "A Shelby Cobra. I'd call her Mercury like the Roman god, and she'd be the same color as the stuff in thermometers; brown leather interior."

Fao-cun whistled through his teeth. "I can tell you've thought about it. Did your Dad teach you all that about mercury?"

"Yeah. We used to have a Periodic Table of the Elements, but he sold it."

Fao-cun grunted thoughtfully.

"What about you?" Oramus asked.

"Me?" Fao-cun removed his glasses. "What do you want to know about me?"

Oramus folded his arms over the side of the bathtub and laid his head down. "Where are you from?"

"That's a good question. I was born in Laos. It's a small nation beside Vietnam."

"That's where the war is happening, right? It's bad, isn't it?"

"Yes it is. It seems I left home in the nick of time. You may have noticed that my last name, Bonfois, sounds French. It is. The French occupied Laos for almost sixty years. If you worked for a French gentleman, as a servant the way my father did, you were not allowed to use your Laotian name. You were given a new one. Thus, my family name became Bonfois, meaning either 'good faith' or 'good time.' Perhaps even 'good liver.'" Fao-cun chuckled. "I'm not sure which the Frenchman intended. It's something

I've always wondered." He inhaled, breathing in memories. "Well, what else do you want to know?"

"Back on the bus in Detroit, you said you'd tell me why that man killed my Dad."

Fao-cun sighed through his nose. "Well, Oramus, I don't think that man wasn't just having a bad day. I believe he's part of an organization. A crime syndicate. That's a group of criminals who make crime a business. This one's called Jungle Tears." Fao-cun cocked his head slightly, pondering where to begin. "Coincidentally, Detroit was the birthplace."

"How did it get there?" Oramus inquired.

Fao-cun wiped his stubbly cheek. "I don't know what to tell you, Oramus. That's just where it was founded."

"Who founded it?"

"Four Negro men."

"So the man that killed my Dad was one of—"

"Jungle Tears' thugs; yes, I believe so."

"How do you know for sure?" Oramus persisted.

"Well, they're certainly not difficult to spot." Fao-cun began to chatter irritatedly. "You know, a man is given a firearm and license to use it freely, then suddenly everyone has to kiss the ground he walks on."

"Why didn't the policemen stop him?" asked Oramus with a hint of accusation.

"Well, they can't be everywhere at once, but I'm sure they're doing their best to catch him. The thing is people are afraid to witness against Jungle Tears for fear of becoming victims themselves," Fao-cun explained. "That's why the thugs' egos are boiling over. They can practically get away with anything as long as they have half a brain."

Oramus sat back in the bathtub. "How do you know so much?"

Fao-cun guffawed. "How do I know so much? I guess that's just part of being an educator," he chuckled.

"I'm ready to get out now." The bathwater was growing cool.

"Okay." Fao-cun stood. "Just pull that plug in front of you and set it on top of the faucet. You can dry off with the towel I laid beside the sink. I'll go get your clothes." From another room in the house, Oramus heard him shout, "Don't dry your hair. It'll be easier to cut wet."

Oramus slowly pulled the drain clog from beneath the water's surface and balanced it on top of the stainless water faucet. The tub belched in response. Oramus looked at his broad reflection in the curvature of the faucet. Rocketing to his feet, he snatched a towel nearby and dried off. Raising his knees high, Oramus carefully stepped out of the tub and waited for Fao-cun to arrive with his clothes. A hand wrapped around the door, clutching a pair of garments. Oramus accepted them, and the hand retreated.

"It's just some briefs and a nightshirt. We'll get you a wardrobe of your own in the morning."

Oramus slipped the briefs on first. The neck hole of the tee shirt nearly slipped off both of his shoulders, and the tail ended at his knees. Oramus gripped the brass doorknob and flung open the bathroom door, feeling a wave of cool air. He observed a chair occupying the middle of the kitchen floor. Fao-cun stood behind with a pair of shining scissors held high.

"Come sit down, so we can get this over with," he said. Oramus approached and slid onto the wooden seat. Fao-cun braced his shoulders against the back of the chair. Violently groping the boy's hair, he mumbled, "Now bear with me. I'm no barber." A constant cringe settled on Oramus' lips as his hair was yanked back into a ponytail. With the initial scissor-snip fell three inches of Oramus' locks. From there, Fao-cun began cutting away bits of hair, merely eyeballing the consistency of its length.

"What are we doing tomorrow?" Oramus asked.

"Well, first thing in the morning I'll go pick up your clothes, so you'll have something to wear. Ms. Allegra volunteered Curtis' old clothes from when he was your age. Then I suppose we'll fetch breakfast somewhere and continue your reading lessons for the rest of the day. Excited?"

"Yeah."

"That's what I love to hear." Fao-cun stepped into Oramus' view and crouched to eye-level. His eyes rushed from one side of Oramus' face to the other. At last, Fao-cun smiled, sending a lanky arm to rub the boy's scalp. "Alright. I'm finished. You can get up now." Fao-cun rose and strolled to a closet behind the dining table to retrieve a broom.

When Oramus stood, cool air swathed his scalp. Placing his palms on top of his head for warmth, he went to coil himself into a ball on the couch.

As Fao-cun swept clumps of wet hair into a brown heap, he asked, "Is the couch okay with you?"

"What do you mean?"

"To sleep on. Will it bother you to sleep on the couch? My bed is only a twin."

"No."

"You know, on second thought, why don't you take the bed?" Before Oramus could object, Fao-cun added, "Not a word. It's final."

~

Fao-cun charged to the front door, his jet black comb-over catching some wind.

"Put on your shoes," he ordered.

The boy slipped into Curtis' old Doc Martens and skipped out the open door.

A shaft of morning sunlight beamed from a window at the end of the corridor.

"Go take a look," Fao-cun whispered from behind him. "It overlooks the campus."

Oramus approached the luminous pane. He pressed his forehead on the glass. Below, a circular courtyard rippled from the roots of a great, gnarly oak. The courtyard was empty save for Curtis trimming bushes around the perimeter. The far end of the courtyard branched into three routes. The right and left routes led to identical, gothic buildings of dark gray. However, the middle route culminated at a grander building than even the administration facility. It was an enormous, cubic structure, crowned with spires at each corner. The solid block was made of sheer stone, seeming to weigh a million tons. There were three rows of windows on each side and a tumorous dome on the roof.

Fao-cun spoke from over Oramus' shoulder. The boy flinched, startled by his presence. "That's the school building, and those two are the dormitories."

"What's that on top of the school building?"

"That's an observatory. You can see the stars from there."

"Up close?"

"Up close." He shook the rapt boy's shoulder. "Come on. Breakfast!"

Oramus blinked and abandoned the sight, eager to enjoy the hearty breakfast he had long awaited.

Six elapsed years

"Turn right here," ordered Fao-cun.

Oramus obediently spun the wheel, clipping a curb with his back wheel.

"Watch it!" Fao-cun jotted down a note on the clipboard cradled in his forearm. "Don't cut the wheel too sharply."

"It was a accident!" the teenager barked back. Several meters down the road he saw a slim bridge browned by rust. "I hate this bridge."

"I know."

Oramus rolled his eyes and scowled out the window. His neck muscles tensed as he squeezed through the narrow bridge. He leaned close to the steering wheel and curled his lips inward. When the vehicle re-emerged on blacktop, Oramus sat back in his chair.

"Don't get too comfortable. Stay alert," Fao-cun warned. He let out a huff. "Did you even see that yield sign?"

"I looked at it."

Suddenly, Oramus felt a cool tickle in one of his nostrils, followed by wetness on his upper lip. He looked down. A few red splotches were rapidly multiplying on the thigh of his khaki pants. Pellets of blood dropped from his face like a leaky faucet.

"Oramus, watch the road!" cried Fao-cun. His arm shot across the console and seized the wheel. He corrected the car, which had been drifting into oncoming traffic. A horn blew.

"My nose is bleeding!"

"Pull over!"

Oramus looked up and regained control of the steering wheel. He licked his lips reflexively to the distasteful flavor of iron. With the aid of Fao-cun's steady hand, Oramus guided the vehicle to the side of the road and parked.

Fao-cun rapidly unbuttoned his shirt and tossed it off. In a single motion he then pulled off his gray, sleeveless undershirt. "Hold this to your nose until it stops. I'll drive us home." Fao-cun began redressing in his button-down.

"No, I can drive us back. Look. I'll just tie this around my head," Oramus scrambled. He wrapped the undershirt around his skull and tied a knot in the back. "See?"

"Oramus, surely you can't breathe like that."

"Yes I can. Please? I want to drive." Oramus looked at him with the most melancholy expression he could conjure.

"Alright. If you insist," Fao-cun ceded. "But if that starts to get uncomfortable just tell me, and I'll take over. Okay?"

"Okay." Oramus ignited the engine, peeking out onto the road over a bloody mask.

~

Fao-cun sat on a large throne. The seat and armrests were spacious. Fao-cun took up little room, thinking two other men could fit comfortably on either side of him. He felt shriveled and spindly, slouching like a beggar. The throne, along with the numerous ornaments hanging all around him, seemed to be made of solid gold. Fao-cun perceived that he was sitting in the framework of a lofty pagoda. Jungle surrounded him on all sides. Directly in front of him dwelt a still pond reflecting the colors of the jungle. A tender breeze floated through the temple from behind, cooling the backs of his ears. Fao-cun noticed a long, thin, gray beard lazily reach out from his chin to grasp the moving air. He didn't remember getting there or why he'd come but remained content to stay motionless and ignorant. The breeze rustled its way through the jungle. The rustling became faint, then queerly doubled back and grew more sluggish and inconsistent, varying from violently shaking trees to quiet, rhythmic stirring of forest debris.

Fao-cun's curiosity heightened. A thin man in a brown three-piece suit emerged into the clearing on the far side of the pond. With only a second's hesitation, the man continued over the pond, taking firm, confident steps on the surface of the water. The pond rippled under the soles of his brown shoes. He reached the near shore and climbed two squat steps into the temple, finally standing no more than a foot away from Fao-cun. The man's suit was not disheveled but remarkably clean without holes, tears, snags or stray threads. His fine, black hair was combed perfectly and his bifocals almost invisible. His shoes were unscuffed. Fao-cun scrutinized them, finding the face of an old man on each polished toe. Looking back up to the visitor's eyes, Fao-cun recognized himself as a young man like seeing a vivid, old picture.

Fao-cun gazed at the visitor for an indeterminable amount of time. His youthful counterpart remained statuesque. Fao-cun noticed a sword in the young man's right hand. He wasn't sure if the sword had always been there or if it had only recently appeared. The hilt was magnificent: red-jewel-and-diamond-studded, its smooth silver merged seamlessly into the gleaming blade. Young Fao-cun raised the sword high above his head and let it plunge.

Fao-cun awoke sitting diagonally in a rigid chair. His hand covered his face and an armrest was lodged between two of his ribs. Drowsily, Fao-cun stirred. He massaged his side and picked up the magazine that had fallen from his lap when he dozed off. Halfheartedly attempting to smooth out the bent pages, he slapped the magazine down on the pile next to him. He surveyed the empty waiting room of the urologist's office. Fao-cun recoiled, and a shriek leapt from his throat at the sight of a plump nurse sitting in the chair beside his. A curly crown of red hair blazed out from under a white hat atop her stark uniform. A cartoonish smile pushed up her round cheeks like a chipmunk.

"You startled me."

"We've finished analyzing your sperm sample, Dr. Bonfois," she chirped.

"And?"

"Good news."

Fao-cun shuddered. "Really?" he breathed.

Fao-cun awoke once more, now in his bed in London. His mind frantically churned to discern fact from imagination. He pitched his covers away, feet connecting to the floor magnetically. He lunged into his closet, attacking a filing cabinet. Fao-cun yanked open the top drawer and scoured through an army of labeled manila folders. When his fingers lit on the folder he sought, he plucked it out and removed a white insert. His dark eyes clumsily shuffled across the paper—a doctor's report. They suddenly stuck as to a flytrap, finding the results section. *Infertile,* he read.

Fao-cun bitterly shoved the file back into the cabinet and slammed it shut. He exited the closet and glanced at his bedside clock. *3:13.* Late or early? Fao-cun chose early. He twisted at the waist and tugged his pajamas. Stepping into his slippers, the professor opened his bedroom door. He tiptoed past Oramus, asleep on the hide-a-bed, into the kitchen. He spun the knob for hot water at the sink and retrieved a cup from the cupboard. His undershirt was soaking in a basin of red water. When the column of running water began to steam, Fao-cun filled up his cup and turned off the tap. Again in silence, the man bent over the countertop, sipping his hot water and watching Oramus sleep.

Five elapsed years

"What is a cult?" Fao-cun strutted behind his potato-colored desk, one hand in a vest pocket and the other tracing a black line across the chalk-caked blackboard. "Yes, Mr. Applegate."

A sporty, sweater-vested young man with his hand raised answered coolly from the fourth row. "A cult is a religious sect, small in number, usually considered extremist."

"A religious sect, you say," Fao-cun reiterated. "Ms. Krauss, what is wrong with Mr. Applegate's definition?"

A studious woman sitting on the far right of the front row spoke. She had a tightly curled mane and a pencil wedged behind her ear. "Erik's definition is too specific."

Applegate shifted in his seat.

"Very good, Ms. Krauss. Would you mind supplying the class with a broader definition?"

"Well, a cult is a group whose beliefs are unusual to the norm."

"Almost, Ms. Krauss. Let's go broader. Have we any Latin scholars in the classroom?"

A stiff, insectoid, neckless student projected an arm from the back of the room.

"Ah, Mr. Alagoz; provide us with the Latin derivation of the word 'cult,' if you please."

The student's voice was as rigid as his body. "I believe 'cult' derives from *cultus* which means something along the lines of adoration?"

"Adoration. So, Mr. Alagoz, would you agree the meaning of 'cult' could include any group that cares deeply for something?"

Alagoz hesitantly responded, "I guess so."

"Therefore, in America, baseball is a cult!" The classroom erupted in a collective giggle. "Let's keep exploring. How many of you have heard of Jungle Tears?" All of the students raised their hands. "You may be interested to know that in Nigeria, 'cult' is the common term for a gang. Considering that Jungle Tears is a gang with roots in Nigeria, is it not appropriate to classify it as a cult?" Fao-cun's lips twitched as he awaited a reaction from his students.

"It began in Nigeria?" one asked, voicing the entire class's question.

"Ah! Yes, yes. It did—kind of. You see, about twenty years ago, four brothers of the Igbo tribe—the Agus—immigrated to America as children, presumably orphans, ending up in Detroit. Growing up there, they were immersed in criminal influences. Within five or six years, the Agu brothers became prominent Detroit gangsters. At that point, in the mid-sixties, they decided to go into business for themselves. And thus Jungle Tears was born," Fao-cun proclaimed with a grand gesture. Then touching his head, "They were smart about it, too." Fao-cun drew a large circle on the chalkboard. Adding a second circle inside the first, he said, "They began hiring thugs—white and black alike—bouncers, bikers, tough guys starved for authority, to do their dirty work: petty drug deals and such. They provided the men with black market weapons, instilling a sense of power over normal citizens. Those men then hired thugs of their own, who, in turn, hired more, and it continued in this manner," the professor taught, drawing smaller and smaller concentric circles. "The Agu brothers essentially set up a feudal system, in which they were the kings. Needless to say, Jungle Tears quickly spread outside of Detroit." He slapped the chalk down. "With each new employee, their spoils increase. Money is always pumped back upriver to the Agu brothers."

Again, Ms. Krauss spoke up. "How did they become so successful in a time when Negroes were so persecuted?"

"I've often wondered the same thing. It's a good question. Perhaps their white subordinates were either sympathetic to the Negro cause, or else they didn't realize who they were working for. If you ask me, the fact that the Agu brothers are both Negro and big-time crime lords was their own little contribution to the American civil rights movement. It was their personal cattle-prod poke in the side of white supremacists."

"I see what you're saying, Dr. Bonfois," chimed Applegate, "but you have to admit it's kind of silly. Today's connotation of the word, 'cult,' strictly affiliates it with religion. Do you disagree?"

"Erik, I'm a theologian. It's my job to agree with that," replied the professor, garnering a few laughs.

"Dr. Bonfois is just trying to bring our minds to the limits of the English language," the studious girl retorted.

"No, no. It's okay, Ms. Krauss. Mr. Applegate is right. This isn't an English class. We're learning theology." Fao-cun strode to the blackboard again, grabbed a piece of chalk and began writing in large capital letters, speaking as he wrote. "A cult is a small sect typically founded in," flashing a glance at Applegate, "but not restricted to, religion." The sentence filled the length of the blackboard. "That is the necessary definition for this class."

When Fao-cun had finished writing, he clapped his hands together, propelling a puff of chalk dust. "Time for lecture," he announced. "Today we will study cults in a religious context. Let's begin with a cult of Roman origin. Nemopatra. Its name comes from the Latin, *anima patrum*, or roughly, 'souls of the fathers.' Men—and only men—of this cult believe their sole purpose is to honor their fathers' spirits. The worshiping process begins at a young age, entailing years of prayer and meditation that lead up to the death of the father. In fact, as an initiation of sorts, cultists often kill their fathers. They see it as a favor, ending their fathers' lives so that their fathers may be honored sooner. Once the father is dead, the subject devotes his life to honoring and worshiping the memory and ghost of the deceased. Remnants of this cult, Nemopatra, still exist today in primitive parts of Southeast Asia, where it reached flourishment. This explains the extreme bastardization of the Latin, for there it was passed down through oral transfer only. Obviously, natives were not familiar with the Latin language. The cult's name was not even written down until a Dutchman recorded it in 1650."

"How did it get there?" mumbled a lean student on the second row.

"Pardon me, Mr. Krand?"

"You said Nemopatra began in Rome. How did it get to Southeast Asia?"

"You want my favorite theory?"

The student scratched his head through trim, wavy hair. "Why not?"

"Well, you've heard of Ferdinand Magellan, the first man to circumnavigate the world."

"Yes."

"And you also know that he was the first European to discover the Philippines."

"Right. That's where he was killed."

"He died there, yes. Whether he was killed is in question. You see, a few months back, archaeologists stumbled upon a lead that could prove otherwise. There's an old Filipino village called Maalindog. In the village records they found several references to a certain hermit, calling him *banyaga*, Tagalog for 'foreigner.' The documents also described him as *putla* or 'pale-skinned.'"

"Magellan?" Krand asked.

"Quite possibly."

"What about his alleged death in battle?"

"If the theory is true, a scam. He very likely could have paid off his crew. Told them to inform the crown of his untimely death. Ordered them to leave him on the island, letting Antonio Pigafetta, the chronicler of the voyage, make up the murder sequence."

"So the battle against Lapu-lapu never happened? Surely the Philippine people would have recorded that."

"It definitely happened. No doubt about that. The end is what we can't be sure about. Following through with this theory, after his crew abandoned him, Magellan may have surrendered to Lapu-lapu and traded all of his possessions—at the time, weapons and armor—for his life. He must have convinced Lapu-lapu to say he'd killed Magellan, effectively enhancing the image of Lapu-lapu and removing the Portuguese sailor from existence at the same time."

Ms. Krauss spoke up. "I don't get it. What's Magellan's motive for erasing himself?"

"Religious freedom," Fao-cun responded.

"You're saying he was a member of this cult"—Krand checked his notes—"Nemopatra?"

"Exactly. I thought that was clear. The man was obviously tired of acting under a façade of devout Catholicism."

"What makes you think he belonged to this cult? Isn't it just as feasible that his crew deserted him and tried to cover it up with an account of his death?"

"Well, witnesses of the hermit claimed that often he shouted the word *ama* in worship and meditation. In Tagalog, *ama* means 'father.'"

Krand sighed. "That does explain the cult spreading to Southeast Asia. Can anything be done to prove that Pigafetta's account is false?"

"Not without written evidence. The only crewmembers to keep some sort of daily journal—that we know of—are Pigafetta and Francisco Albo, and both vouch for his death."

"There are other theories, right?"

"Of course. There are always other theories. Some think Nemopatra didn't begin in Rome at all. Some say it goes back further than that. They claim a participant of Alexander the Great's campaign delivered the cult to Southeast Asia. Anyway, the point is that Nemopatra has always been here; scattered and quiet but unmistakably active. It has remained hidden from society for centuries, like a figure in a dark corner that you know is there but just can't see. A chameleon of cults!" Fao-cun shouted, thrusting a crooked finger in the air. "If the theory we were discussing is true, then Magellan spent his entire life hiding the fact until he landed in the Philippines." Fao-cun cleared his throat. "Now let us contrast Nemopatra's secrecy and longevity with a few modern cults."

~

A chattering bell blared through the school, signaling students to collect their notepads and textbooks.

"We'll finish this discussion next week!" Fao-cun yelled above the ringing. "Remember your term papers are due on the 16th!"

The students filed out of the classroom, book-bags over their shoulders. One lingered in front of Fao-cun's desk as the professor packed his briefcase.

"Do you enjoy giving me a hard time, Oramus?"

"What do you mean?" asked the smirking student.

"I would have gotten through this lecture if it wasn't for that blasted 'why.'"

Oramus laughed.

Unable to retain his false seriousness, Fao-cun joined his laughter. "You don't have any more classes today, do you?"

"No."

"Then let's get lunch." Fao-cun's fingers tightened around the handle of his briefcase, and the two men strolled out of the classroom.

Oramus was now taller than Fao-cun; and due to eleven years of generous feeding, he was toned and muscular. The hallway in the school building was a sea green terrazzo with pine specks. Oramus ran his finger along the slick, marble wall as they journeyed for the staircase, Fao-cun exchanging salutations with passing colleagues. They entered a stairwell, where their heels clacked like Gatling guns descending. They left through a side entrance a flight below.

Oramus asked, "Where to?"

"I was thinking we'd go to Borg's."

"Sounds great. We haven't gone there in a while."

The men walked to a street corner and crossed a barren roadway with long, swift paces. A blue neon sign reading *Borg's Bread and Butter* rested above a frumpy diner. The pink neon sign of its even rattier-looking neighbor read *Borg's Beers and Brawls*. Fao-cun pushed through the door to the diner, Oramus behind him; a tiny bell jingled. They sat at a booth beside an expansive window painted with hand and nose smudges. There were no other customers in the room. A face peeked from the kitchen.

"Borg! Dr. Bonfois is 'ere!" burst a female cockney voice.

"Who?"

"Dr. Bonfois!"

"Oh, that ol' codger?" An obese figure barreled through the kitchen door. Oramus was immediately reminded of how disproportionately scrawny the man's legs were compared to his podgy upper half. The small-town tycoon came striding up to their table, drying his hands on a grease-spotted apron. He smacked a great hand into Fao-cun's and shook vigorously. "So 'ow is the ol' Falcon, eh?"

"Fine, fine. How about the notorious, black-haired Swede?"

"'E's good! Very good!" the cook wailed. "You don't come visit me as much as you used to."

"Well, Borg, I was starting to get fat. Had to lay off England's best for a while."

"That never stopped me!" Borg thundered, patting his belly. "And Oramus! You're getting to be quite the colossus, aren't you? Built for rugby. So what can I get you two rambunctious billy goats?"

Fao-cun ordered first. "Meatloaf, scrambled eggs and coffee, black."

"Alright. An' you?"

"How about fish, asparagus and a cup of tomato soup?"

"To drink?"

"Water."

"You got it. It'll be comin' righ' up. Now you two be'ave, and I'll bring your grub out in two shakes of a lamb's tail."

"Thanks, Borg."

Borg sauntered to the back, whistling.

Fao-cun propped his chin on laced fingers. He stared Oramus warmly in the eyes. "Oramus, your senior year is almost over. Do you feel ready to survive by your own hands, and put your degree to good use?"

Oramus took a deep, silent breath. "Actually, Fao-cun, I do have plans, but they don't exactly involve my degree."

"And? What are they?" asked Fao-cun dryly.

"You've heard of the League for International Auto Racing?" Oramus tried to sound casual.

Fao-cun tightened his jaw muscle. "I have heard of it."

"Well, the League holds races all over the world, and the racers are of all nationalities. It's really a cultural gem; it celebrates diversity and the global community," he pitched, adding tentatively, "And I'd like to make it my career."

After a brief silence, Fao-cun began to laugh quietly. "You've been privileged enough to receive a college education, and you're throwing it away to pursue auto racing?"

"I'm not throwing anything away, Fao-cun," Oramus defended. "That's the beauty of education. The degree will always be there if I need it."

Fao-cun exhaled through his nose. "In this League of yours, the racer provides his own vehicle, correct?"

"Yes," Oramus conceded.

Fao-cun scratched his eyebrow. "How do you plan to buy a car fresh out of college?"

"After I graduate, I'm moving back to the United States to find a sponsor," Oramus answered candidly.

"And how will you pay the sponsor?"

"I'll get a small job until I start winning races." Oramus laid his hands flat on the table. "In American dollars, the standard prize for winning a race is five thousand. Second prize is twenty-five hundred, and third is one thousand. Now say I do two races a month every year. Half of them I place, the other half I don't. I average second in the placing half. That's 30,000 dollars! The average American makes less than twenty."

Fao-cun wagged his head doggedly. "Oramus, you can't count on yourself winning that often. What if you don't place at all?"

"I know I can do better than that, Fao-cun," Oramus insisted, pounding the table.

"You've never even raced before!"

"'If you're dedicated and passionate about something, you'll do it well.' You said that, remember?"

"Yes, but"—Fao-cun paused, exasperated—"racing?"

"You know how passionate I am about this. It's been my dream since we first met."

"Why haven't you mentioned this plan to me before?"

"I guess I imagined you reacting like this."

"It's April of your senior year. Do you blame me for reacting this way?" Fao-cun smiled helplessly.

"No."

"Good. I don't think you'd react any differently if you were in my place."

"I know you're only worried about my well-being. And I promise, if I'm not successful, I'll drop it and find a sensible job. You have my word."

Fao-cun leaned back in the booth and stared out the window. Oramus studied him. Shoots of gray were beginning to sprout at Fao-cun's sideburns. Small, defined wrinkles budded at the corners of his eyes and mouth. Almost all of his features pointed to aging. His irises, however, flitted with vivacious thought.

Both men stayed silent until Borg brought out their lunch.

"'Ere we go. A fish sarnie, soup, asparagus and water for the lad. Minced steak, eggs and coffee for the ol' Falcon. Anythin' else you needin'?"

"No thank you, Borg. This looks great," said Fao-cun.

"If so, jus' 'oller."

"Will do."

"Grub up."

Fao-cun dabbed a chunk of meatloaf in a pool of ketchup and chewed briskly. Next, he moved to devouring the eggs. Without taking his eyes from the plate, he muttered at a pause, "You have my blessing."

~

Fao-cun waited for Oramus in the foyer of their apartment. The new college graduate came stumbling out of the bedroom with two suitcases and a satchel on each shoulder. He stopped at the oval doormat, face-to-face with his mentor.

"Is that everything?" asked Fao-cun.

"Yep. This is it."

"Good. Then let's hug here, so we don't make a scene at the airport," Fao-cun chuckled.

Oramus bent his knees slightly to let down the suitcases. The pair embraced.

Fao-cun reminisced, "Can you believe it's been eleven years?"

"It doesn't feel like it's been that long at all. That's over half my life."

They broke partially, and Fao-cun cupped his hand around the back of his pupil's neck. "Oramus, I want you to know I love you like a son."

"I love you, too, Fao-cun. I don't think I could ever begin to thank you for what you've done for me."

"I've given you all the advice I have. Now it's your responsibility to apply it."

"I couldn't have asked for a better handbook."

Releasing Oramus from the hug, Fao-cun smiled. "If your heart is in racing, so is your fortune. You'll do well."

"But I've never even raced before!" Oramus teased.

"You've been an excellent student in everything you've undertaken. Racing should be no exception! I expect visits, remember."

"As soon as I can afford the plane ticket."

"Let's hope that doesn't take too long."

Oramus bent over to again take hold of his suitcases. "We should go. My flight leaves in an hour and a half."

"You're right." Fao-cun opened the door, let Oramus tromp through, then flicked the light switch and followed him out. Slowly, the door clicked shut.

~

Oramus vigorously slapped the screen of the trailer-home in front of him. Once again, he checked the address beside the door and verified it with the one written on his palm. The door squealed open. A tall, flabby man in his fifties stood behind the screen. Tufts of brown hair stuck out from the pits and V-neck of his black muscle shirt.

"Can I he'p y'?" he asked from under a grizzled mustache.

"Hi," Oramus began, partly taken aback. "I'm looking for a Mr. Richard Wiley. Am I—"

"Yes, y're in the right place." The man pushed open the screen door. "Come on in."

The interior reeked of chewing tobacco. Oramus followed his host into the kitchen.

"Call me Rick," he said, walking.

"My name's Oramus Krand."

The man turned at the kitchen table and offered his hand. "Pleasure."

They shook.

"Can I get y' a beer?"

"I'm fine, thanks."

Rick plopped down onto one of his dining chairs and raised his leather cowboy boots onto the table. The soles were caked with red dirt. "Y' can wipe that look off y' face, boy. If it gets stuck like that, I'll do no business with y'."

Oramus gulped. "I'm sorry," he chuckled. "I guess I just didn't expect—"

"—a wealthy big-wig like me to be livin' in a doublewide. Yeah, I get that look a lot." Rick shrugged. "I live comfortable. I got what I need. The way I figure it, a man'd be smarter to spend his fortune practically, don't y' think? Most people don't understand that a man can be wealthy, who don't live in a mansion."

"I respect that, sir."

"Good. Now pull up a chair. I assume y're the kid I got a call about?"

"Yes, sir." Oramus grabbed a dining chair and seated himself. "I'd like to request your sponsorship for a racing career."

"Well, I'll have to see y' race, of course."

"Of course."

"How much experience y' got?"

"Uh, none, sir."

Rick stared for a moment. Finally, a grin broke. "Y're serious?"

"Yes, sir. I am."

"How old are you? Nineteen? Twenty?"

"Twenty-one, sir."

"And, le' me guess, y' did good in driving school, saw a race on TV and thought it looked easy, right? Won a few go-cart races and now y' think y're a pro?"

"Actually, sir, I've never raced. And I took driving lessons from my guardian. But I can drive. I mean, that's what matters, right?"

"What makes y' think y' can compete? This is a professional sport."

"Well, I have a good work ethic, I learn fast, and I like cars."

Rick stood, running fingers over his buzz-cut scalp. "A man'd have to be out of his right mind to sponsor you, son."

Oramus rose to meet him.

"Lucky for you, I know from experience sane men just don't make it." He walked to a key rack on the wall and tossed Oramus a set. "We're goin' to the track. Let's see what y' can do wi' Wilma."

Rick led the youth through his den adorned with racing trophies to a back door. It opened onto a carport housing a diesel truck and a dirty, unpainted, armor-plated stock car. The car's filthiness paled next to its collection of gaping dents, scrapes and gashes.

Holding out an arm like a magician presenting his money-trick, Rick introduced her. "Meet Wilma, y're new practice vehicle. Wilma, this is Oramus, y're potential driver-in-training. Y'll have to climb in through the window," he mentioned, mounting the pick-up. "Just follow me."

Oramus appraised the battle-scarred tank named Wilma. He took hold of her roof and clambered in feet-first. The bare, metal seat was clearly not installed for luxury. After tackling the complex array of straps and buckles, Oramus stuck the key into the ignition and twisted strongly. A resonant grind thundered from Wilma's belly. Oramus backed out of the carport behind Rick, grinning like a child.

They trekked a couple miles down a narrow, gravel road through a grove of scattered, squat hardwoods until they reached a spacious clearing. Rick parked beside an oval, red-dirt racetrack and got out of the truck. Oramus pulled up next to him.

Palming a stopwatch, Rick shouted, "Toe the line! Fifty laps!"

Orange cones outlined the in-and-outside boundaries of the racetrack. Oramus inched through a gap in the cones, up to a horizontal line of white spray paint. He wiped sweat from his palms, leaving two damp stripes on his jeans. Peering through the passenger window, he spied Rick posing with a shotgun at his hip. Oramus readied his hands at ten and two, foot over pedal. The gun clapped; his sole flattened the gas pedal, and the car lurched forward.

~

The local barbeque restaurant was noisy with country-western tunes blaring from wall-mounted speakers and beered-up Texans shouting at one another from across the room. Oramus sat alone at a four-chaired table. He scratched the plastic, red-and-white-checkered tablecloth. Everything was overwhelmingly American. Oramus would only ever-so-often grasp that he was on a different continent, having to choke down the same afterthought every time. He couldn't let the prospect of finding Lex trump his financial stability.

The waitress left the kitchen through a swinging door. Her dirty blonde hair was pulled back, but a loose strand furiously whipped the side of her head as she sped around a labyrinth of tables, heading in Oramus' direction. She stopped beside him, notepad in hand and retrieved a pencil from the knot of her ponytail.

"Hi," she said. "Welcome to Pig-In-A-Blanket. What can I get you to drink?"

"Sweet tea seems popular around here. Can't say I've ever had it. We drink hot tea where I'm from."

"And where's that?" she inquired, intrigued by the unfamiliar cadence in his voice.

"England."

"Wow." She smiled, showing a wide set of pearls. "Well, you're right. Sweet tea is the preferred drink around here. I recommend it."

"Then that's what I'll have."

"Okay. Coming right up." Having jotted down the order, she paced back to the kitchen, still smiling. Oramus watched her leave, admiring the fit of her pale blue uniform. Moments later she reappeared holding a tall, red cup and returned to Oramus' table. She put the cup down in front of him. Ice tapped its flimsy, plastic walls. The waitress plucked a straw from a pouch of her immaculate apron and placed it on the table. Oramus unwrapped it immediately and took a swig of the beverage.

"So what do you think?" the girl asked.

"Finally, I know what the craze is all about."

"Good," she laughed. "Are you ready to order?"

"Your suggestion worked once. What do you recommend this time?"

"My favorite is the pulled pork. Do you like pork?"

"Sure. I'll try that."

"Okay. Fries or chips?"

"Chips—uh—fries," he stumbled. "Sorry. English thing."

"Okay," she chuckled. "Will that be all?"

Oramus remembered an expression he'd often heard over the past few days. "Yes ma'am," he replied.

"Great. I'll be right back w—"

"Hold on," Oramus interjected. "Do you happen to know a Rick Wiley?"

"You kidding me? He's a celebrity around here."

"For training racecar drivers?"

"Yep. Word is he's got a new trainee. No one knows much about him yet. But you know how small towns are." The waitress smirked.

Oramus extended a hand. "I'm Oramus."

"Gwen Alby." She shook.

"Sorry—I don't mean to keep you; I know you're at work."

"That's okay. But I should probably keep moving. It's busy tonight."

"When do you get off?"

"I work late during the week, but I'm free on the weekends."

"Great." Oramus smiled.

Gwen stifled a giggle. "I'll bring your sandwich out in a few minutes."

"Looking forward to it."

The waitress smiled and fluttered her fingers as she walked away.

Oramus eyed her for the rest of the evening. He even ordered a cup of coffee after his meal as an excuse to stay longer. By the time his coffee vanished, the place had quieted down considerably. Gwen approached Oramus' table one last time.

"Refill?"

"No thanks. I'd better head out."

"Okay then. Here's your ticket." She handed him a slip of paper. "Just bring it to the register."

Standing, he said, "Sure thing." Before Oramus turned to leave, the pair locked eyes. "I'll see you 'round?"

"Definitely."

As Oramus walked away, Gwen reached down to collect the tip. A few black scribbles on the face of a one-dollar bill snagged her attention. The marks read, *6:00 Sat. Outside.*

~

Oramus sat in the passenger seat with one hand on the shiny, blue hull of Rick's diesel pick-up, wind tweaking his budding, brown curls.

"Where are we going?" he asked.

"I need to make an order at the shop," Rick responded. He often ordered spare parts for Wilma at the local garage.

"So why do you need me here?"

"Hold on. First, Mama Wiley's comin' over for dinner tonight. I'm fixin' chili and calf fries. Would y' like to join us?"

"Sure, that sounds great. What, exactly, are 'calf fries?'"

Rick cackled. "I ain't tellin' 'til you try 'em!"

"Oh no," Oramus laughed.

Rick finished his whooping. "Well, anyway, she's comin', and I was hopin' y'd be there to meet her. My mother's very dear to me."

"Yeah, I'd love to meet your mother, Rick."

"Good. Now the other thing I wanted to talk to y' about—there's a race in Mexico City nex' month. I think it'll be a nice chance for y' to get y're name out there."

"You think I'm ready for that?"

"Close. We're going to be working hard over the nex' few weeks. Y' got me?"

"Absolutely."

"Y' got fine talent, boy, real fine talent. Y' jus' got to be refined. That's my job." Rick flicked on his blinker. "I'll supply the seventy-dollar entry fee, the pit crew and the car; and all you have to do is race. And race good." As Rick turned into the auto shop parking lot, Oramus realized why they were there together. "Now as I understand it, y' want a silver AC Cobra?"

～

Oramus sat in a dining chair, sipping a beer bottle. At the stove, Rick churned a five-gallon pot of chili with a wooden spoon. Occasionally, he would bring the spoon to his lips and nibble, after which he would unfailingly add seasoning.

A rapping sounded at the screen.

"There she is." Rick tapped his spoon on the pot's edge and laid it across the top. Wiping his hands on his jeans, he said, "Come on."

Oramus followed Rick to the door. Rick slung it aside and pushed the screen open for his snowy-maned mother. She held a white casserole dish covered with aluminum foil.

"Hey, Mama!" He embraced her tightly with one arm and kissed her on the cheek.

"It smells good in here!" She shoved the dish into Rick's plump gut.

"What've you done?" he asked, cradling it reflexively.

"It's jus' some bread puddin'."

"You didn't have to do that, Mama."

"Of course I didn't, but if I want bread puddin', by gosh I'm going to make it. This mus' be, Oramus."

"Yes, ma'am." Oramus stuck out his hand.

"Put that away, and hug my neck!"

Oramus bent down to hug her wafery body. "It's great to finally meet you."

"You too, son. Rick hasn't stopped talking 'bout you!"

"Alright, alright. Into the kitchen," Rick grumbled.

Mama Wiley leading with short, methodical steps, the three of them shuffled into the kitchen. Rick set the bread pudding on the counter; then he and his mother gathered around the stove, while Oramus returned to his seat at the dinner table.

"How's the chili?" asked Mama Wiley.

"It ain't quite perfect yet, Mama."

The elderly woman drifted to the counter and opened a drawer. Her arthritic fingers pulled out a silver spoon. "Let me taste." She hunched over the pot, spooned a dab and docked it between her dentures. "Where's your onion powder?"

"In the cabinet, but—"

Mama Wiley started for the cabinet. "That'll fix it."

"But, Mama, my chili recipe don't call for onion powder!"

"Maybe that's why it ain't perfect."

"Mama," he whined as his mother approached the chili, unscrewing the lid on a shaker of onion powder.

She gave it two firm thrusts into the vat.

"Y're not even goin' to measure it, Mama?"

"It's fine!" Mama Wiley nabbed his wooden spoon, stirred the chili and offered Rick a bite. "Taste that." Rick dropped his jaw in obedience. She shoved the spoon into his mouth, accidentally decorating the corners of his lips with excess. "You don't have to say it; it's delicious." She dipped the spoon back into its chili bath.

As the rickety lady wobbled toward the dining table, Rick flashed Oramus an amused glance. "Let's eat these calf fries while the chili cools," he said.

When Mama Wiley sat down, Rick served a basket full of deep-fried nuggets. The old woman savored a piece while Rick nonchalantly tossed one in his mouth, chewing fast. Oramus fearfully guided his hand to the basket and took one. He watched as it muscled toward his lips. His tongue receded. The morsel crunched between his incisors.

"You eat mountain oysters?" Mama Wiley exclaimed. "Rick said you's born in the north."

Oramus halted his chewing. "Yes ma'am."

"Lord have mercy! I ain't never met a Yankee brave enough to eat the testicles of a bull!"

Oramus swallowed; Rick grinned. "Are you serious?"

The men erupted in laughter.

Mama Wiley looked at Rick. "You mean you didn't tell that boy what he was eatin'?" she snapped.

"We had a deal! I promised to tell 'im as long as he'd try one first!"

She turned back to Oramus. "Well?"

He took another calf fry and held it up. Rick and Mama Wiley cheered as he ate the chunk whole.

Rick set the table. He carried over the tub of chili and ladled everyone a serving, beginning with his mother. Finally sitting down, he dove into a bowl.

"Good news, Mama. We saw a 'Help Wanted' sign at the shop today."

Oramus added, "What's funny is Rick and I had just been talking about me finding a job this morning."

"I tell you, that boy was just a-complainin' about not bein' able to find work," Rick prodded.

"How was I supposed to know they had an opening if they didn't put an ad in the paper?"

"So they hired y'?" Mama Wiley inquired.

"On the spot," said Rick. "Apparently Dominic's boy has moved off someplace, so they were down a man."

"When do you start, son?"

"They'll train me next week, but I don't start with pay until the Monday after."

~

Oramus sat in a rented sedan outside of the Pig-In-A-Blanket. His watch read 5:56. The car was silent save for Oramus persuading himself that he would spot Gwen at any moment. He looked at his watch again, expecting 5:58 but still seeing 5:56. Mentally pacing, he muttered, "Calm down. It's not even six yet." The sky was gray by now except for a crown of pink sunlight that seemed to sit on the roof of the restaurant. Oramus checked his watch once more—*5:57*. When he reset his eyes on the sidewalk, he saw a girl in a blue jean jacket scanning the area like a radar. He opened his car door and sprang out in a single motion. Folding his arms on the car's roof, he shouted, "Gwen!"

The girl snapped her head to Oramus. She waved in recognition and ambled up to the car.

"Hey."

"Hop in." Oramus ducked back inside the vehicle. Gwen opened the passenger door and did the same.

"Where are we going?" she asked.

"I don't know. Where are the local hang-outs?"

She smirked. "Is this a date?"

"I guess that depends on where we go."

"Well what did you have in mind?"

"Do you have any suggestions? We both know how good you are at making those."

"We're not too far out of Austin. There's plenty of things we can do there."

"A date it is then—to Austin." He pulled away from the curb.

"You know how to get there?" Gwen asked.

"For the most part. I may need a little help."

Before long, they passed a large sign on the highway, reading *Pickens, Texas. Come see us again!*

"So have you always lived in Pickens?" Oramus ventured.

"Mhm," she grunted.

"You like it here?"

Gwen sighed. "Well, it's home," she said. "Can't say I wouldn't like to go somewhere else, though. No one should be stuck in the same place for nineteen years."

"Are you in school?"

"Community college." She met his eyes. "You?"

"I just graduated. What's your major?"

Her voice rose. "I don't know. I should though, right? But I've never really had anyone to talk to about careers and education and stuff. You know what I mean?"

Oramus chuckled. "Not really. I grew up with a college professor as my legal guardian."

"Lucky you."

"Seriously, don't stress out over it. It'll come to you."

A suspicion animated her eyebrows. "I don't think you ever told me your last name."

"Oh, did I not?" Oramus teased.

Smirking skeptically, Gwen replied, "No, you didn't."

"Krand."

"I knew it! You're Rick Wiley's new trainee."

"You caught me." Oramus grinned.

"Why didn't you tell me at the restaurant?" Gwen punched his arm.

Oramus shrugged playfully. "It was more fun this way."

The pair laughed aloud.

Gwen said, "Rick's a nice guy, isn't he?"

"Oh yeah." He tossed her a glance. "You know him well?"

"We go to the same church." Gwen scrunched her face in thought. "And I think he and my Dad were good friends. I found a picture of them together when I was digging through the attic."

"I met Rick's Mom last night," Oramus spouted. "He had us both over for dinner."

"She's a sweet woman."

"Funny, too!"

"So what exactly do y'all do every day, you and Rick?"

"Well, he takes me out to his track and times me, gives me pointers; we discuss pit stop strategy. Things like that," Oramus explained.

"All day?"

"All day. Until I start my new job on Monday. I'm a new mechanic at the auto shop."

"Dominic's?" the girl inquired.

"Yeah."

"Is there that much to learn about racing?"

"You'd be surprised."

"When is your first race?"

Oramus took a breath. "Next month. Mexico City."

"You think you're ready?"

"I hope so. What's important is that Rick thinks I am."

"Well, good luck," she chirped.

"Thanks." Oramus turned his focus to the bright green road signs. "How much farther is the Austin exit?"

Pointing down the road, Gwen replied, "Not far. Just a few more miles."

"What's the plan when we get there?"

"Have you eaten?"

"Nope. You hungry?"

"Starving," she blurted hungrily.

~

Oramus' northern-bred skin baked within a navy blue jumpsuit under the Mexico sun. He admired the glint of rays reflecting off his new Cobra's roof. The automobile was exactly as Oramus had wished—deep silver paint with two cobalt stripes stretching from bumper to bumper.

From a wide stance, arms folded, he stared intently at the artful creation, entranced by its reality. *Hello, Mercury*, he thought.

"It ain't going nowhere," said Rick from his lawn chair under the tent a few feet away.

Returning from his dreamy state, Oramus replied with a chuckle, "I know. I guess I just have to make sure it's real every now and then."

"Well, I paid for it with real money," Rick laughed.

Part of Oramus groaned, knowing how long it might take to repay Rick for the investment. However, it was a diminutive notion beside his elation.

"Everything's ready to go here. Y'ave time to take a short walk around if y' want."

"Will the other racers mind? I mean, is that—polite?"

"Naw. They shouldn't care. Pro'ly won't even notice. But if y' do run into a butthead, let me know."

"Will do." Oramus strode past his new car, tracing Rick Wiley's signature on the hood as he passed; the trainer didn't demand much advertising.

Oramus began to roam the preparation area. The long strip housed several racecars, bustling pit crews, trailers, sponsor flags and puffy, white tents. Oramus strolled, gawking at the competition and cradling a white helmet in the crook of his arm.

A particular pitman captured his attention. He was a kind-faced, muscular, black man in his prime, hauling tires from a trailer and stacking them on the ground nearby. He sported a mid-sized afro. The pitman hadn't noticed Oramus' approach and re-entered the trailer for another load of tires. When he returned, Oramus could barely see his face over three thick tires. The pitman's eyebrows jumped in surprise, quickly followed by a greeting smile.

"Scared me," the pitman chuckled.

"Sorry about that."

The pitman waltzed past Oramus, bringing a strong whiff of rubber. The sleeves and torso of his jumpsuit swayed behind him.

"Name's Oramus Krand. I'm Number Four."

Back muscles bulging, the pitman dropped his armful and spun around; he clapped his hand to Oramus'. "Kip Swanson. I'm Rudy Vincenz's pit captain. He's Number Six. How can I help you?"

"Oh, I don't need anything. I'm just here to make conversation. Press out the pre-race jitters."

"Okay, that's cool," Kip licked his lips. A couple of wiry, gray hairs swirled out from his temples. Oramus estimated he was midway through his thirties.

"So you from England, man? I like the accent."

"I actually live in Texas now. You?"

"Houston, baby. What part you from?"

"Austin."

"Alright, alright. How long you been racing?"

"This is my first race. I've been training for a couple months."

"That's not long."

"I know." Oramus took a deep breath, his self-esteem tearing.

Kip broke down into a chuckling fit. "Don't sweat it, man. I'm just messing with you. Instinct can take you a long way in this sport. If you got good reflexes, ain't no telling what you can do."

"Rick keeps telling me that."

"Rick Wiley? Rick Wiley's your sponsor?"

Oramus nodded.

"Then what're you so worried about? Look—your coach has trained nine racers since the League began, and all nine had unbelievable records. Raz Fogarty was undefeated! You're the new chapter of a legacy, my friend." Kip licked his lips again. "If I know Rick Wiley like I think I do, you may win this race yet, baby."

"Well, we'll see about that. It's interesting—of course, I've heard about Rick's history, but he doesn't mention it much himself. He's only mentioned Raz once or twice."

"You're lucky. If you aim to follow through with this career, he's got the knowledge and experience you need."

"What about your guy? Vincenz. Tell me about him."

Kip scratched his head and groaned. "Tough to say. We're business partners, you know? Don't want anything slipping in a public arena."

"I see," Oramus comprehended.

"I will give you this: Rudy's a first-class racer. He can handle a steering wheel with the best of 'em." A harsh, electronic beep shot through the area. "That's your cue, my man. Time to hit the starting line."

"Alright, well, it was nice meeting you."

"You too, brother."

"What's your telephone number in case I ever find myself in Houston?"

"Can you remember it?"

Oramus affirmed.

"Two, two, two, one, seven, twenty-one."

"Got it. Do you have an answering machine?"

Kip nodded. "Don't think twice about giving me a ring, understand?"

"Thanks."

"Good luck on the track."

"And you at the pit."

Kip winked as Oramus departed. When he arrived back at his station, Rick motioned for him to get in the car right away. Oramus swooped in and secured the straps across his chest. Flicking the engine into vivacity, he fell into the line of racecars. They paraded into a stadium to a symphony of applause. The numbers one through twelve were stenciled in a diagonal row on the track. Each racer proceeded to his corresponding mark, Oramus stopping at *four*. After all the racers had taken their places, a capped man in a striped shirt appeared at the sideline. He raised an air horn.

When the horn blared, Oramus' boot crushed down on the accelerator. He launched into a speeding current, looking at three cars ahead of him: a silver Mercedes-Benz 300SL Gullwing, a lime AMC Gremlin and a bright yellow Ferrari 250 GTO. The latter led the bunch. It was piloted by Rudy Vincenz.

Four-hundred-ninety-nine laps ticked away faster than Oramus could notice them. At every pit stop, he kept his hands on the wheel and carefully regulated his breathing. Throughout most of the race, he had oscillated in and out of fourth place. He now had only one lap to snatch third. The Ferrari and the Gremlin were still first and second. The car Oramus had to beat was a candy apple Lancia Stratos. He was on its bumper. Entering the final turn, he boldly moved to the inside lane and advanced before the Stratos could merge in front of him. Oramus gunned forward through the fresh channel, the little orange hand on his speedometer surging well into the hundreds.

~

"So I started trucking it." Oramus' eyes lit, and his knuckles whitened on the steering wheel. "The Stratos was steadily taking up less and less space in my window, and before I knew it the finish line was behind us! I was so excited, I literally jumped onto Rick's shoulders."

"He was happy, too?" Gwen inquired.

Oramus spoke through spurts of laughter. "Are you kidding? You couldn't have jack-hammered the smile off his face. He said to me"—imitating Rick's voice—"'The rookie takes third place by a nose!'"

"What about Kip?" Gwen asked like a child listening to a bedtime story. "Did he come congratulate you?"

"Well, since Rudy Vincenz won first, it must have been difficult for him to get away, but he eventually made it over to our tent."

"Are you going to visit him in Houston?"

"Actually, I was thinking about going this weekend. Do you want to come?"

"I have to work, but don't let that stop you." She touched Oramus' shoulder. "What are y'all going to do?"

"I don't really know. It may not even work out." Oramus shrugged. "We'll see what happens."

"Yeah." Gwen twisted in the car seat, leaning her ear on the headrest. She watched Oramus fixedly. "Finish your story."

"That's pretty much it." He continued with less enthusiasm. "Afterwards, Rick treated us to drinks at this cantina. We crashed in a motel and came home yesterday morning."

A silent moment passed. Gwen exhaled and watched Oramus drive. She stroked the brown, leather car seat and admired the snazzy, chrome dials on the radio console. "Why do racers in the League race such expensive cars? Aren't you worried they'll get banged up?"

"Not really. It's a gentleman's sport; you don't get aggressive on the track. The penalty is disqualification, and you're liable for any damages you cause to another racer's vehicle."

"What if you damage it yourself?"

"It's a risk." Oramus shrugged. "There's not much the League can do for you then." The conversation came to a halt when the ethnic, baritone voice of a radio disc jockey piped through the Cobra's speakers.

"Good evening out there, everybody." He talked in a quiet, mellow tone that demanded attention to hear it, as if he was trying not to wake someone dozing in the studio. "It's Sphinx talking, and it's 9:15. You're listening to 152.5 FM. You just heard Gaspergoo, and coming up next we have Leroy and the Fine China, followed by our nightly Rhythm and Blues segment. Enjoy." An acoustic melody drifted into the car almost unnoticed like the trickling of mourners to a wake. A cracking, nasally voice began to sing.

> *I was walking down the road*
> *and let me tell you what I saw.*
> *I saw a poor, old farmer*
> *getting hassled by law.*
> *Then I looked out in his pasture*
> *to see how the crops were doing,*
> *but on those yellow stalks of corn*
> *a plague of bugs were chewing.*
> *The farmer came to me and said*
> *The good times is gone.*
> *So I looked on down the road,*
> *and I moved on.*
>
> *I moved on, I moved on.*

Shooting trespassers with a slingshot
'cause I can't afford a gun.
I moved on, I moved on.
Eating duck 'cause we're out of swan.
I looked on down the road,
and I moved on.

I came upon a hound dog,
chain embedded in its neck.
It looked as if in all its years
it had not eaten a speck.
It pawed my shoe. It begged and whined,
but not a morsel could I give.
I had to turn my face away,
wond'ring how the dog would live.
If it could have spoke, it would have said
The good times is gone.
So I looked on down the road,
and I moved on.

An interlude of strings, bells and woodwinds spilled from the speakers.

"I have another question," Gwen hazarded.

"What is it?"

"It's about your brother." She paused as one does after taking the first step on to a rickety bridge. "I was wondering why you've never gone after him, especially now that you're back in the States."

Oramus became distant. "Actually, not long after we were settled in England, Fao-cun reported a missing child to Detroit police, but there wasn't much they could do with just an over-the-phone description. Fao-cun tried his best, but it just didn't work out. Sure, it was hard for me, at first, to grasp that I would probably never see my brother again; but you grow out of those feelings, make new friends. At some point, I just accepted it."

"And you don't want any closure?" the girl probed in disbelief.

"Of course I do. I'm human. But at this stage in my life, I can't afford to just run off and search for him. Maybe one day when I'm steady on my feet and have some months to spare; but for now I just have to keep doing what I've done for eleven years—" Oramus' gaze pierced her eyes. "—stop thinking about him."

> *At last I came to a place in the road*
> *Where I knew the city was near*
> *'cause a big, green sign in front of me*
> *Said "The good times is here."*

~

Oramus strolled down the balcony of a Houston apartment building. It overlooked a rectangular swimming pool five levels below. Oramus' eyes jumped from door to door until they lit on *5U*. He stood still and knocked on the green door, noticing several exposed layers of paint.

"Hol' up!" shouted a familiar voice from inside. A chain slid, and the door opened. Kip Swanson stood in the entryway wearing another white muscle-shirt and picking his afro compulsively.

"Hi there," Oramus greeted.

"Hey, man." They shook hands, and Kip swung the door wide. "Come on in. Make yourself at home." He gestured to a sitting area comprised of a low table between a couch and a nicked, wooden chair. "I'll be right back." He slipped into a narrow corridor that trailed off to the left.

As Oramus approached the couch, Kip yelled, "You thirsty? I got water, milk, Coke and rum!"

"I'm fine," Oramus responded.

"How about a sandwich or something?"

"I'm fine," Oramus repeated. He sat down on the couch, sinking backward in the seat bucketed by age. A tidy chessboard commanded the table before him. Every piece was precisely centered in its square. Oramus leaned in for closer scrutiny. He found the lustrous marble well-dusted and scratchless.

Suddenly, Kip reappeared from the compressed hallway holding two cans of soda in one hand and a short glass of amber rum in the other. "You play?" he asked, intrigued.

Oramus wobbled his hand.

With a devilish grin, Kip plunked into the wooden chair. He set one can of soda on a coaster and one on the carpeted floor at his side; the glass of rum remained in his hand. "I got you one anyway. You ain't got to drink it."

"'Preciate it." Oramus tapped the lid and opened the can with an echoing pop.

"I'm black," Kip asserted.

"I'm sorry?"

Kip pointed to the chessboard. "Is that cool wit' you?"

"Oh, yeah. Fine," said Oramus.

He made his first move. Kip reacted without blinking, as if it were routine. Oramus followed posthaste, working to maintain the pace. Still, Kip moved innately like he had played the same match a hundred times before. Oramus countered. Kip moved. Oramus countered. Captured in a whirlwind, Oramus found himself in checkmate already.

"Mate," Kip stated blandly. Without hesitation, he began resetting the pieces. "You're moving too fast, man. Take your time. This game isn't a race." Kip swigged his rum. "And don't let me aggress you like that. You're playing way too defensively. Again?"

"Sure."

They started over. Oramus slouched, drumming his lips. This time, he dissected each option exhaustively before laying a finger on the board.

By the time the second match was over, Kip's rum was depleted along with half of his soda.

"How many times are we going to play?" Oramus asked, taking his third sip of the afternoon.

"Until you beat me," Kip replied smugly.

Oramus smiled and returned his dewy can to the coaster.

~

His queen rooted proudly on Kip's second row, Oramus carried his last rook to the enemy base, the final stroke in the trapped king's defeat.

"At last!" Kip shouted, flinging a hand across the table for Oramus to slap. "Good game, brother. It only took thirteen of 'em."

Oramus raised his arms victoriously. He wiped his eyes and checked his watch. "It's nine. I'd better hit the road."

"Alright, man."

"Can I use your bathroom before I go?"

Kip rolled up a large bag of potato chips and pointed. "Yeah, man. Down the hall; on the left." He started crushing soda cans beneath his heel as Oramus entered the cramped hallway.

The hallway was not deep. When Oramus reached the end, he viewed a cracked door to his right. Inside, he glimpsed a wall-mounted rack holding a military-grade automatic rifle next to a shotgun and a machete, which dangled by a leather strap. Below, on a rectangular card table lay scattered ammunitions and two pistols of largely differing size. Oramus promptly turned left into the bathroom, fearing he had gawked too long.

When he returned to the living room, Oramus noticed that the chess set was in rigid order again; Kip lay on the couch, fingers over his eyes. Sensing Oramus' reemergence, Kip sat up.

"Didn't know you were a gun collector," Oramus chuckled.

"Shit. Was my door open?"

"A little, but I was just joking; it's really no big deal." Oramus waved dismissively.

"Sorry about that," Kip apologized, shaking his head. "I've been meaning to get rid of them."

Oramus remained still and quiet, expecting further explanation.

At length, Kip continued. "I used to be involved in some bad stuff, but I'm done with it now."

Feeling discomfort encroach on the room, Oramus jumped in. "Yeah. It's none of my business."

"So you out?" asked Kip.

"I should. I'll be late getting back as it is." Oramus eyed his watch for emphasis.

Kip offered a final handshake. "Enjoyed having you over, man. Next time you can improve your wins-losses ratio."

"Thanks for having me. And I'll be practicing."

Kip laughed drowsily. "That's right."

Oramus opened the door, welcoming in nippy air. "See you 'round." He waved, keys loosely jingling around his middle finger.

"Peace, man."

～

Smoke rose from Lex's lips to blend with the overcast sky. The young man's absinthe eyes glowed in the dullness, shamelessly staring at three men across the street from his vantage point against a graffiti-tattooed building. The men conversed with beer bottles in-hand. One was a scruffy white man who sported a Detroit Tigers baseball cap and jacket. The second was obese with protruding lips, dark, sunken eyes, and black hair just long enough to be messy. He wore a tight, gray tee shirt. The third was tallest and broadest. His melon head was shaved smooth save for two bushy eyebrows with skin a gray-brown. Lex thought he may have been Turkish or something. The brute flaunted mammoth biceps in a black, sleeveless undershirt. On the right bicep, he displayed a tattoo of an immense baobab tree. Its trunk covered his whole upper arm; roots crept down past his elbow, and foliage fanned out over his right shoulder. The three were more than friends hanging out on a sidewalk; they were gangsters, Jungle Tears thugs. The Turk's tattoo was a marking many of Jungle Tears' men opted to bear. Lex had often heard the goons talking business. Over the past weeks he had eavesdropped on their daily conversations, but today he was just watching. The threesome was gathered shortly beyond a hotdog vendor soliciting his wares to a woman and her toddler. Taking another drag on the cigarette, Lex ran a finger down the zipper track of his cotton jacket. A pair of tiny, silver boxing gloves hung from a chain against his bare chest. Lex had defeated many navy men in the ring to earn those. They had a nickname for him there: Yahtzee; inspired partly by his surname, partly by his luck, but mostly because when he scored in the ring, he scored big. Thirty-five of his thirty-eight wins were by knockout.

Once the mother and son had left the hotdog vendor with their lunches, Lex spit out his cigarette, touched the cold gloves and began crossing the street.

The hotdog vendor smiled as Lex approached his pushcart.

"Three hotdogs," Lex ordered.

"Sure." The vendor put three buns in a paper boat and plopped a pale, grayish hotdog in each one.

Lex snatched the boat and stepped away from the cart.

"Hey, quarter each." The middle-aged vendor's face feigned toughness.

Silently, Lex walked around the cart to where the vendor was standing. With his free hand, he delivered a hard slap to the vendor's ear and shoved him to the concrete. Then, placing his hand on the edge of the cart, he wrenched it from the ground and sent it skidding into the street. Finally, he shot a heel into the stunned vendor's stomach. Without missing a beat, Lex gazed to the group of men he'd been observing. He had captured their attention. Following a bout of predatory eye contact with each one, Lex advanced on them.

"You boys want some hotdogs with those beers?" he asked nonchalantly.

After a second, the man in baseball attire spoke first, identifying himself to Lex as the leader. "What the hell are you trying to prove, kid?" he asked in a gravelly voice.

"I want in."

"In what?" barked the Turk, challenging him.

"Hell do you mean 'in what?' In the circus. What do you think?" Lex barked back.

"We don't have any openings," said the baseball fan.

Lex dropped the hotdogs and let the jacket slide off his arms. He projected his fist straight into the Turk's nose, followed by a powerful kick to the sternum, thrusting Goliath to his back. Lex pounced on him. Pinning the man's arms with his knees, Lex mercilessly slugged his face again and again. He bared his teeth, appetite unquenchable, ferociously hammering the helpless skull between his knees. Like a relentless machine: raising and plunging his fists, his shoulder, chest and back muscles twinging and contorting. The continuous pounding made an audible, slushy *whack* like jogging in mud. *Whack, whack, whack, whack, whack, whack.*

"Alright. Stop. That's enough," commanded the leader. Lex barely slowed. *Whack. Whack. Whack.*

"Hey, are you dense? I said that's enough!"

Lex forced his arms to relax. His heaving torso swayed, off-balance. He inhaled a lungful of air and pushed himself to his feet. Knuckles stained red, he peered into the man's eyes under the brim of his cap. Spurting the words between violent breaths, Lex said, "Now you have an opening."

"Listen, kid, this ain't an after-school club. You can't just sign up. You got to be invited."

Lex looked at his necklace. A couple specks of bloods decorated the silver boxing gloves. He popped the gloves in his mouth, sucked and spewed them back out. "Invite me," he spat venomously.

One elapsed year

Oramus scooted his chair closer to the kitchen table. Its legs screeched across a linoleum floor. Hands cupping a full coffee mug, Oramus inhaled the rising fumes. Beside him, Gwen rubbed his nape; he felt the prick of her icy wedding ring. They uncommittedly watched a television screen positioned on the countertop. The sports news channel featured a heavyset, gray-haired fellow speaking energetically. The initials of the League floated above his shoulder. "The League of International Auto-Racing Semi-Finals are next Monday. Racers to look for are, of course, Rudy Vincenz, the current champion, and a relatively fresh competitor from Austin, Texas: Oramus Krand. This rookie's only been around for roughly a year and already has an astounding record of 23 placing to 9 non-placing."

"Let's turn this off. I don't need Walter Melin reminding me of my own judgment day," Oramus grumbled.

Gwen picked up a remote and pressed the wide, red power button. "Why are you so nervous? Listen to what the man's saying. He's naming you as one of the most dangerous competitors."

"I know." Oramus rubbed his face with both hands. "That doesn't help. If anything, it makes the pressure worse." Gwen grabbed his hand and squeezed affectionately.

Her knuckles blanched. Oramus looked her in the eyes and smiled. "Don't worry about me, honey. I'm always nervous before a race. It's just that my career depends on this one." He paused. "And if that's the cake, wait'll you hear about the icing," he joked grimly.

"What?"

A cooking timer dinged jarringly, cueing Gwen to leave the table and peer through the oven window. She held the neck of her ivory robe together with one hand.

"I got a call from Fao-cun this morning," Oramus announced.

"And what did he have to say?"

"He was—angry," Oramus recounted.

"Angry? What for?" She turned her back on the oven.

"Hurt's a better word, I guess," he admitted. Oramus rubbed his forehead and swept a hand through his hair. "It's my fault."

Gwen glided into the chair beside him. "That's ridiculous. What could you have done?"

"I think that's the point." Oramus sighed. "I don't keep in touch like I should," he confessed. "Now that racing's really taken off, it's hard to squeeze in a letter or a phone call, much less a visit." He inhaled shakily. "I don't know what to do now. I've hurt his feelings."

Gwen cradled his hand and rubbed it with her thumb. She kissed the corner of his mouth. "Nobody's Superman, baby." She seized eye contact with a hand on his cheek and gave him a wisp of a smile.

"Something weird happened, too." Oramus stared into his coffee. "When I picked up the phone, he said, 'Does Oramus Krand still live here?'"

~

"Yes, Fao-cun. I still live here." Oramus sighed.

"That's odd. I never get any calls from this number anymore."

"Listen, Fao-cun. I'm sorry. I can explain—"

"What is it that keeps you Oramus? Your career? The one I supported? All I asked is that you wouldn't forget me."

"Fao-cun, I could never—"

"I've seen you twice since you left London. Christmas and the wedding; both times I flew to you. Your lack of consideration nauseates me." Fao-cun's voice was electric. "I don't deserve this, Oramus. I'm your father."

"What?" It leaped from Oramus' throat like a flying fish.

"What?" Fao-cun's voice was suddenly tiny. "That was a mistake." The sentence was in territory between statement and question. "I have to go," he sputtered.

The dial tone followed like a shadow.

~

Leaning on the oven, Gwen scrambled for the right thing to say. "Just forget it ever happened," she replied, uncertain if she'd found it.

Oramus scoffed. "Yeah, okay."

Silence fell; Oramus slurped his coffee.

"Are you coming up to Detroit with me on Sunday?" he asked.

"Sorry, baby. I told you I can't. I have a German exam on Monday."

"That's right." Oramus rotated his coffee mug. "It will be my first time back in Detroit in twelve years. You think he could still be there?"

Gwen drew a long breath. "You shouldn't dwell on that." She bent down to check the toast. Snatching a dish towel from the achromatic fridge, she opened the oven, heat masking her face. An aroma of cinnamon and toasted bread permeated the room as Gwen slid out the pan and laid it on the table. Oramus took a slice in each hand and plopped them onto his plate.

Gwen sat, and they began eating. "When are you going to Kip's?"

"Actually, I thought I'd invite him up here for dinner."

"That's a great idea." Gwen sipped her coffee.

"Haven't run it by him yet." Oramus took another large bite of toast.

"I'll dig out my Mom's old recipe book."

"Did I tell you he's moving?" Oramus inquired.

"No," she chirped. "Where to?"

"Didn't say."

"You think it has to do with him quitting Vincenz's pit crew?" Gwen held the mug to her lips and blew.

"It's likely. I guess we'll find out at dinner."

They continued eating in silence. When she finished, Gwen brushed her hands off above the plate and took a final gulp of coffee.

"I have to get ready for class." She stood and kissed her husband's temple.

~

Oramus' eyes pinged open to a rotary phone rattling by his ear. He took a moment to get his bearings. Spying the unfamiliar desk and mirror, Oramus realized he'd awoken in Detroit's Kingdom Suites. Finally, he snapped the berserking telephone to his ear. Reading *7:49* on the digital clock at his bedside, he grumbled, "Hello?"

A thick, female, Indian accent responded, "Hello, Mr. Krand. There are two gentlemen in the lobby who would like to speak with you."

"Who are they?" Oramus asked, yawning.

"Sirs, what are your nam—" Her voice was cut off.

Suddenly, a deeper, severe voice began. "Gambol's Sandwich Shoppe, 1015 Woodward Avenue, at exactly 11:59 a.m. or—" Another interruption ensued.

A third voice entered, distanced from the telephone receiver. "Damn brother!" The voice became clearer—sly and charming. "Good morning, Mr. Krand. Excuse us for waking you."

"Good morning," Oramus mumbled, wearing a confused look.

"On behalf of Mr. Igwe Agu, I'm calling to request your audience for lunch at Gambol's Sandwich Shoppe, located at 1015 Woodward Avenue."

"What?"

"Astounding, I know." The voice said haughtily. "How does noonish sound?"

Oramus docked the receiver and rubbed his eyes. Tossing back the linens, he sat up and swung his legs to the floor. Just as his toes touched the carpet, the telephone rang once again. Oramus yanked the receiver to his ear a second time.

"Yeah?" he fussed.

The smooth talker answered. "I wouldn't advise you do that again, Mr. Krand, for you know not the consequences." His voice was less friendly but just as debonair.

"Consequences?" Oramus' tone betrayed a trace of fear.

"Let's not dwell on those just yet."

"What do you want?"

"We've been over this, Mr. Krand. Weren't you listening?"

Oramus didn't answer.

"Igwe Agu has invited you to lunch."

"I can't. I have somewhere to be."

"I'm sure any conflicts can be resolved with ease. So if you'll kindly meet him around noon (though fashionably late is not preferred)—"

Oramus spoke loudly into the phone. "You said there would be consequences. Am I being threatened?"

"Look, Mr. Agu just wants to make a new friend. Is that too much to ask?"

Oramus slid his fingers through his hair. "Yes. I have a very important—"

"As if simply meeting the man isn't enough, you need more incentive?" The speaker paused. "Well then you should know your wife will be there. Noon at Gambol's Sandwich Shoppe, Mr. Krand. Don't call the police."

Dial tone.

The telephone was glued to Oramus' ear for several seconds. Suddenly, he thawed and sprang to his suitcase. He stabbed his legs into some jeans; stepped into shoes. Grabbing his coat from the rack, he scurried out the door. People in the hallway viewed a wild man in a wrinkled tee sprinting sockless to the elevator; arms blindly seeking a sleeve-hole. He collided with the elevator door, pressing the button frantically. As the door sluggishly drew open, Oramus stumbled inside.

He tore into the lobby, eyes scouring for the caller.

"Ma'am!" he shouted to the flustered, Indian receptionist. "Two men just called my room. Where did they go?"

The receptionist pointed to the entrance, where a motionless revolving door awaited. Oramus darted outside. Seeing no dubious candidates ambling the sidewalks, he spun back into the lobby; his cheeks and ears flamed. Oramus observed a wall clock behind the front desk—almost eight. He thrust a finger at the receptionist. "Call the police."

"Sir?" the woman answered.

"Police!"

She picked up the receiver and dialed. Oramus gestured for the phone. He tucked it in the crook of his shoulder, signaling for a pen and paper; she slid them over the counter. Oramus freed the pen cap and started jotting down notes.

"Detroit Police Department."

Oramus spoke, winded yet controlled. "Yes. I am at Kingdom Suites. A man just phoned my room and threatened to hurt my wife unless I show up at Gambol's Sandwich Shoppe at noon."

"Okay, sir. Did the man indentify himself?"

"No, but he said he worked for Igwe Agu."

"Okay, sir. We'll dispatch an officer to the Kingdom Suites right away."

"Thank you." Oramus handed the receiver back to the disturbed receptionist and staggered to the nearest chair. When a trim police officer finally swaggered into the lobby after what seemed like half an hour, Ormaus jumped up and met him by the door.

"Officer."

"You called about the threat?"

Oramus nodded, and the policeman took out a notepad.

"What's your name?"

"Oramus Krand."

"You said there was a phone call?"

"Yes."

"Can you describe the conversation to me?"

"A man told me I had to be at Gambol's Sandwich Shoppe at noon, or he would hurt my wife."

"Describe her? What's her name?"

"Gwen Krand. She's blonde, brown eyes, average height, thin, pretty."

"Do either of you have any enemies?"

"No. I don't. I don't think she does either. None she's ever told me about."

"Describe the caller." The officer hardly looked up from his notepad.

"Okay. Well, he was kind of a smart aleck. Said he worked for Igwe Agu." Oramus jolted. "Actually, there was another one before him. A meaner one."

The policeman smirked.

"Do you have any idea who they are?"

"I think so."

"Okay. What should I do?"

"I'd say your best bet is to show up at the deli at noon. We'll follow you there, of course."

"The guy said 'no police.'"

The officer chuckled. "They always say that. But he knows we're coming."

"Is there anything I should do in the meantime?"

"Go get cleaned up," advised the calm policeman. "Read a book, or watch some TV. Whatever it takes to get your mind off the situation." He smiled courteously. "Thanks for your cooperation. I'm going to head back to the station."

Oramus nodded, brow in furrow.

The officer departed briskly through the revolving door. Oramus floundered for a few seconds before turning toward the elevators.

Back in his room, Oramus immediately began to strip and hopped in the shower, still shaken. Pulse thumping like a helicopter rotor, Oramus inhaled and exhaled, spewing water droplets from the shower stream. Gwen should've been back in Austin. He hadn't thought to call home. What did Agu want with him? The weight of the impending race began to settle on his mind. He knew he would miss it.

~

Oramus' knees danced under the restaurant table. His fingers drummed the tabletop. It was three minutes until noon.

Oramus' nerves peaked as three proud, black gentlemen sauntered through the glass doors. He almost immediately pointed out the man with whom he spoke over the telephone. He was a short fellow in a borderline-tacky, orange-brown suit with straight hair pulled back in a pigtail. Next to him walked a taller, bulkier, flattopped man in a black muscle shirt and sunglasses. In front strode the obvious leader of the trio, a shorthaired, broad-faced man, jacketed in ankle-length, black leather, who was tugging at the fingers of his gloves. He showed Oramus a wide, bullfrog smile.

"Mr. Krand, I presume." He pulled a pocket watch from inside his coat. "Eleven fifty-eight. You're early. Hope I didn't keep you waiting." He chuckled heavily.

Oramus held his tongue.

Agu sat down across from Oramus. His neck popped as he jerked his head to the side and boomed to the aproned sandwich-makers, "My usual, fellas." Agu's companions stood at each shoulder. "Oramus is it?" Agu asked. "Am I pronouncing that right?"

Oramus affirmed. "Mr. Agu, how exactly is my wife involved in this meeting?"

Agu lifted a massive hand from the table. "Hold on just a second. Not until everyone's been introduced. These are my friends." He pointed his thumb over his right shoulder at the small man. "I believe you spoke with Asp this morning on the telephone."

Asp stroked his thin mustache and soul patch and winked at Oramus. Agu's thumbs switched. "This is his brother, Adder." Adder stood like a palace guard, unbudging. "They're only half-brothers. Same Momma."

"Now if you'll please—"

"Sorry to interrupt again," Agu interjected. "Have you ordered anything?" He arched his eyebrows jocosely.

"No. I'm not hungry."

"Nonsense. Hey fellas," he yelled to the employees. "Another one of those for my pal." He looked back at Oramus. "Continue."

"Mr. Agu, I've had a stressful morning, and it's done more than drain my patience, so is my wife okay, or isn't she?"

Agu watched him squirm. "Well I simply couldn't wait to meet you. My connections are very important to me."

"Well knowing me won't be worth much after today. I'm missing the semi-finals for this."

Agu shrugged. "You'll get as much publicity either way. Besides, I'm booked for weeks. This is the only available lunch I have until August," he laughed.

Oramus grinned. "Forget it. You're bluffing." He took a single step out of the booth before a low chant from Agu's mouth froze him.

> *Georgie Porgie, puddin' and pie,*
> *kissed the girls and made them cry.*
> *When the boys came out to play,*
> *Georgie Porgie ran away.*

Agu's friendly smile was unbroken. "Sit down," he ordered.

"Why?" Oramus demanded.

"So that's what you insist on getting at, is it? Here I was hoping we could have a pleasant meal like comrades." Agu nodded to Adder. The muscular bodyguard turned mechanically and walked outside.

Oramus sat once again before Agu, whose face had lost all its jollity. They remained silent until Adder reentered escorting Gwen, gagged and tied. Oramus clenched his teeth. Adder handed her off to his brother.

Meanwhile, Agu remained a statue.

"Let her come sit with me, for Christ's sake!" Oramus exploded, voice cracking.

"She's fine," Agu declared, cut off by the chiming of the door.

A graying man, appearing on the brink of fifty, strode in wearing an unbuttoned Hawaiian shirt and jeans with a gun at his belt.

Agu smiled. "Ah, well if it isn't Little Jack Horner. To what do I owe the pleasure, Chief DiRosa?"

"What do you mean, Iggy?" the man replied. "I'm just here for a sandwich." He took a seat at the table across from them.

Agu snapped his head back to Oramus. "I assume he is your doing?"

"Don't blame him, Iggy," the police chief interjected. "What would you do if I called with your wife at gunpoint?"

"You know damn well what I'd do," Agu sniggered. He pulled a long, white smoke from inside his coat and perched it between his lips. "Besides, Mrs. Krand isn't at gunpoint. In fact, I think she's enjoying herself. What do you say, Mrs. Krand? Having fun?"

Gwen tried fruitlessly to rip herself from Asp's claws. "Oh yeah, boss," said Asp, "she's having a ball."

"Where the hell is my Reuben?" Agu moaned, looking to the counter and finding it vacant. "Looks like the employees evacuated." He lowered his voice. "Are you afraid things are going to get messy, Chief?"

"With you, Iggy, they always do," DiRosa answered at equal volume.

Agu looked up thoughtfully. "They do, don't they? Funny." He struck a match for the cigarette.

"Laugh now, Iggy; but one day it'll bite back. Every freight train's got to pull into station sometime."

Agu laughed heartily. "Thank God for that!" he bellowed, blowing a gust of smoke. "If not, we'd just roll right on into the ocean!" He began to mutter another nursery rhyme, even less audible than before.

> *There was a crooked man, and he walked a crooked mile.*
> *He found a crooked sixpence against a crooked stile.*

Oramus snapped like a mousetrap. He lunged over the table, where Igwe's mighty palm launched him back like a springboard. DiRosa instantly unsheathed his firearm and aimed it at Agu's head, simultaneously becoming the focus of Adder's pistol. Agu's eyes were ever-trained on Oramus, and he whispered, "Jack be nimble." Oramus clutched the first item in his reach—a glass ketchup bottle. He threw himself at Agu, swinging for his skull. The club landed once, twice, three times; Igwe rolled to the floor, insensible. Adder faltered, and DiRosa shot him through the chest. Gwen, having wiggled free of her ties, turned on Asp and began scratching at his eyes. He instinctively pulled a keen, crescent blade and jabbed it into her abdomen. Asp pushed her away as she crumpled and retreated in panic.

Oramus clambered over the booth to his wife, tears surging.

"Do you smell that?" DiRosa asked. "Gas." He turned to the kitchen. "They left the grill on." His eyes fell on the table, where Igwe's cigarette lay, still smoking. "Get out, get out, get out now!" He sprang to Oramus and threw him at the door, stooping to take Gwen in his arms. "Out of the building!" he roared to Oramus.

DiRosa caught the helpless, brown eyes of the crime lord on his way out. He slurred:

> *Row, row, row your boat gently down the stream.*
> *Merrily, merrily, merrily, merrily.*
> *Life is but a dream.*

Oramus and the police chief charged across the street. They dropped to the sidewalk, DiRosa trying his best to shield Gwen's body. Heat suddenly enveloped him, as if he were naked beside a bonfire. Tiny fragments of glass trickled off his neck. DiRosa kneeled and checked the woman's pulse, grasping for a walkie-talkie with his other hand. He pressed the device to his lips, ruffling his gray mustache.

"I need paramedics at the deli right away!" Gwen's stomach was painted red. He pressed his hand where the shirt was most opaque.

Oramus pounced to his wife's side, accidentally knocking the chief off balance. "Gwen! Gwen! Baby! Can you hear me?"

"She's alive, Mr. Krand! She's alive!" DiRosa shoved a forearm across Oramus' chest. "An ambulance is on the way. She'll be alright, but I need you to get back."

Surveying the region, he spied the garish escapee lying face-down under a hefty officer and smiled. The smile withered, looking back on the blood that now gloved his hand.

~

Oramus slumped in a dark room, lulled by the beeping of a heart monitor. He watched the rise and fall of Gwen's stomach as she slept, envisioning the wound beneath her blanket. The pillow rumpled her hair partially. Oramus pressed his forehead; the day had given him a migraine. A nurse cracked the door and poked her face inside. She mouthed, "Doctor wants to see you."

Dr. Calvin Hulda waited by a circular reception desk. As they approached, he nodded to Oramus and dismissed the escort. The handles of his eyeglasses burrowed between flaps of skin.

"How are you, Mr. Krand?"

"Fine."

"It's good news." Dr. Hulda smiled. "She'll need to stay with us for a few days, but they'll be alright."

"Who?" Oramus inquired.

"Pardon?"

"Who's 'they'?"

Dr. Hulda nudged his glasses and blinked rapidly. "Your wife and the—" Embarrassment halted him again. "Sir, are you aware that your wife is pregnant?"

~

Oramus sat in sweat at Gwen's bedside. His belly groaned and bubbled like a cauldron. All he had eaten in eighteen hours was a cup of Jell-O. He now fiddled with the spoon to keep his fingers at work. There was a rustle on the hospital bed.

"Oramus?"

Rising fluidly to his wife's bedside, he murmured, "How do you feel?"

"Fine." She smiled and closed her eyes.

Oramus kissed her forehead. "Go back to sleep."

When he began to straighten, she pulled his shirt. "No, stay."

"Gwen," Oramus began, "Can I ask you a question?"

She nodded.

"Why were you in Detroit? I thought you had a mid-term."

"I wanted to surprise you."

Gwen realized a sting in her stomach; her face disfigured in horror.

Oramus touched her cheek. "It's okay. It's okay," he soothed. With a warm smile, he added, "I know about the baby. The doctor says he's fine."

Gwen relaxed and dozed off again.

~

Oramus deposited coins into the pay phone in the hospital lobby and dialed the number scribbled on the back of his hand. He glanced around while the phone rang, seeing two women, one very old and the other middle-aged, headed for the main exit. The younger woman seemed to be in worse shape than the elder. She hobbled toward the door, one hand holding her purse and the other clutching the old woman for stability.

The ringing ceased. "Chief DiRosa speaking."

Oramus plugged his free ear. "Hi, Mr. DiRosa. This is Oramus Krand."

"Oh, Mr. Krand. How's your wife?"

"She's doing well. She woke up this morning very alert and she just went back to sleep." Oramus huddled in the pay phone cubby for privacy.

"Good. How about you? You getting any sleep?"

"A little. Have you made any progress on the investigation?"

"We searched Agu's penthouse. There was a message on the answering machine that explains everything. Bad news is we can't identify the caller."

"What did it say?" Oramus inquired.

"I have the tape with me. Why don't you just listen for yourself? I'll load the cassette in my tape deck and hold the phone up to the speakers."

"Okay."

Oramus heard the muffled clinking of the tape entering the player. "Hey, Iggy. It's me," said a male voice. "I need a favor. I need you to keep someone busy this weekend.

The specifics are in your P.O. box. This is important to me, so I'll pay handsomely if you're interested. If not, let me know ASAP. Uche won't help me; he flat-out refused. Maybe you should talk with him. I don't know; you know how he is. Anyway, talk to you later, Iggy." A loud hang-up noise followed.

"Still there?" asked the chief.

"Yeah, I'm here," Oramus affirmed. "Did you check his post office box?"

"It's empty. We turned the penthouse upside-down, but nothing turned up. If we don't find those instructions, we won't have any evidence on the caller."

Oramus sucked his lips. "Denny, can I ask you something?"

"Anything," the chief replied.

"There's a question that's been swimming around in my head." He hesitated.

"Oramus, you can ask me anything. I mean it. I'll answer you man-to-man."

"Am I in trouble for, you know, Agu?"

"What are you talking about? He stayed in the building voluntarily. I told everyone to get out, and he didn't. It was suicide." DiRosa's voice was blunt. He seemed to wink at Oramus from across the telephone wire.

Oramus chuckled lightly and dabbed the corner of his eye, unsure whether to thank him or to play along.

"Everyone knows he was batshit crazy," the police chief laughed. He soon swallowed the joviality. "Listen. Dying is the best thing Igwe Agu ever did for this city."

"Yeah," Oramus breathed.

"Well, you ought to get back in there with your woman," DiRosa continued. "Be thankful you've still got her. Lord knows what I'd do without mine. I'll keep you updated on the case," Denny declared, wrapping up. "You might call me back later this afternoon."

"Will do." Oramus hung up and glanced around absently, bearing back to Gwen's room.

~

Lex thoroughly examined the windowless, octogonal room around him. He had been left waiting for twenty minutes now. The cozy chamber appeared to serve as a private study or library. Laden bookshelves covered five of the eight walls top-to-bottom. The east wall to Lex's right framed a stained, wooden door, rich and thick, which led to the rest of the manor. On the north wall sat a lavish, royal blue bergère beneath a tall, hooked floor lamp. An antique globe the color of parchment stood beside the chair. A sky-colored chaise longue rested behind Lex with a cylindrical pillow at one end. Lex leaned back on two legs of the Victorian armchair. Looking up revealed four crossbeams supporting a domed ceiling. A small, rustic chandelier hung where the crossbeams met. Directly below, in the center of a round, glossy table basked a single hefty volume. Its blonde binding jumped out from the slab of uncreamed coffee. Lex leaned forward; an ornate border and majestic title were engraved on the cover: *The Collected Works of Chinua Achebe.* Lex massaged his right shoulder which the leaves of a baobab tree now decorated in black ink.

At last, the gold knob on the eastern wall twisted, heralding the entrance of an imposing gentleman in a tailored, gray suit. The snug room seemed even smaller with him in it. Lex recognized the man to be Nwanneka Agu, the third-born of the Agu brothers. One of the first things Lex researched coming into Jungle Tears was textbook information on the Agu brothers. The youngest in his late-twenties was Amadi Agu. He conducted business in and out of Moscow. Few knew much about the man. Even fewer had met him. Lex understood that Amadi didn't visit the United States regularly. He was more inclined to stay atop a throne in his cupcake-topped Russian palace.

Second youngest was Nwanneka, a resident of Paris and drug-trafficker of Western Europe; he had just broken thirty years of age. Nwanneka was known for an outspoken fondness of his brothers. Many would say he spent more time in Detroit and Moscow than in Paris. However, the city was nonetheless a major influence on his character. He was fluent in French and a patron of many French museums. In addition, a large portion of his business consisted of the export of exotic and expensive French wines.

Igwe Agu was the second-born son. He was physically the strongest and most martial of all four brothers. Guns and ammunition dominated his trade. He sold them—and used them. He used them more than his brothers would have liked. Igwe was the only brother to stay in Detroit, and eventually its citizens and newspapers began naming him a "terrorist." Some years ago he had begun killing people seemingly for the hell of it. There was never enough evidence to arrest him, though. Police could only get their hands on bottom-tier criminals. That was the nature of Jungle Tears; guppies were always plentiful. Lex had met Igwe before. He seemed somewhat of a mental case. He wasn't crazy—maybe the opposite.

The eldest, Uche Agu, was by far the most elusive of the bunch. He was not associated with any particular region, nor did his brothers often see him. However, on multiple occasions, his three younger brothers attributed their early survival to Uche's ingenuity. Supposedly, he snuck them on a boat to America, led them to Detroit and found their niche in the black market. Of all the brothers, Uche intrigued Lex most. The man was a mystery, which Lex was determined to solve.

"Please keep your seat," Nwanneka insisted upon entering the room. His African and French accents bled through his speech. "We may skip the introductions; you know who I am, and this report," he said, thumping a manila folder, "will tell me everything I need to know about you." The dark-skinned business man sat across from Lex in an identical Victorian armchair. He opened the folder and began reading. "So your full name is Alexander Dolan Dyce, correct?"

"Correct," Lex solemnly affirmed.

"Well, welcome to my home, Mr. Dyce," Nwanneka declared with brief, friendly smile.

"Thank you, sir."

"I hope your travel was free of headaches," he asserted, still skimming the document.

"Entirely, sir."

"Is this your first time in Paris?"

"It is." The visitor's breath was inaudible; neither finger nor toe fidgeted a hair's-breadth.

"You were in the U.S. Navy for two years."

"Correct."

"And you've been with us for—?"

"Twelve months."

"Twelve months," he repeated. "No education," the boss continued as from a list.

"None formally, sir," Lex avowed, "but that doesn't mean much."

Nwanneka released a bass chuckle, accompanied by a toothy grin. He closed the folder and laid it flat on the table. "Do you know who recommended you?"

"No, sir."

"Dante Garvey? Detroit Tigers fan; throaty voice."

"Yes, sir. I know him."

"He's been with us since almost the beginning. Quite a veteran. I take his counsel seriously."

"What's he recommended me to do exactly?"

"Yesterday I received a telephone call from a Detroit jailhouse. An associate, Asp Louche, used his only phone call to inform me of my brother's murder."

Lex suspected as much, having been swept off to Paris immediately following news of Igwe Agu's death.

"The culprit's name is Oramus Krand."

Still no surprise to Lex, for he had read the newspaper article; however, the version he knew was about Agu's "suicide."

Nwanneka spoke firmly and gradually. "Do you understand what I want you to do?" His dark eyelids pulled back, and he fired Lex a bludgeoning stare.

"Retribution?" Lex's nonchalance bordered on pleasure. "It's what I do."

"Good." The larger man straightened in his chair. "Target his friends and relatives—as many as you can. I'll pay five thousand a head. But stay away from Krand and his immediate family. I have plans for them. Understood?"

"Understood, sir. And a question, if I may."

"Of course."

"What will happen to Detroit?"

"I will assume responsibility of the Detroit market," Nwanneka pledged. "It's a valuable city—and my sister-in-law may need some company."

"So is that everything?"

"Unless you have any more questions."

Lex began standing.

"Wait," Nwanneka interjected, holding up a massive palm. "You'll be working alone?" His tone betrayed the question for a command.

Lips curling, Lex responded, "The only way I can."

"Well then. Happy hunting."

~

Lex knew him immediately. He even wore the same fringe-sleeved jacket and eye-patch. The only change was his reddish-brown hair, which had grown thinner and greasier. Lex parked his Jeep on the damp, gravel pier overlooking Lake St. Clair. The one-eyed man stood on a small ridge above the bank. He was lighting a cigarillo.

Lex glanced at the newspaper on his passenger seat dated 1971. An article was circled below the man's picture. *Eberley Sentenced Six Years For Battery*. He should have been serving life for the murder of Ellis Dyce. With a sneer, Lex threw open his car door and got out.

Shoes crunching on gravel, Lex approached the man.

"You got my message," he called out.

The man looked over his shoulder so that his one good eye was fixed on Lex. "That's a stupid observation," he sniped, cigarillo still in his mouth. The lone blue eye scanned Lex up and down. "What do you want?"

"There's a Tears job I need your help on," Lex asserted.

"How do you know me?"

"A recommendation."

"Really," he blurted. "That's strange. I haven't worked for Tears in a long time."

"I know," Lex followed bluntly. "The job pays well. I know you need the money."

The middle-aged ruffian grunted and sucked his teeth. "And you want to work with me," he stated with a hint of disbelief.

"Yes. Does that surprise you?" Lex toyed.

The man turned to face him. "Well, I mean—" He paused, flushing. "You're young."

Lex stiffened his shoulders.

"I figured you'd want to work with men your own age, that's all."

"Are you incapable?"

He puffed his chest. "Well, no. I just meant there are cultural differences between the generations is all. Cultural differences."

Lex spoke coldly. "Frankly, sir, I agree with you, and I'm not looking to be your friend. Can you help me get the job the done, or can't you?"

The old bully took a long drag of his cigarillo and smiled. "Yeah. I can do that." He chuckled, spewing smoke in puffs like a steamboat. "What's your name, kid?"

"I'd appreciate it if you addressed me with the same respect I address you with, sir," Lex stated defiantly.

"Alright then. What's your name, *sir*?" He made little effort to disguise the sarcasm.

"Lex."

"Lex what?" the bully pried, squinting his eye.

"Lex What will do just fine for now."

"Alright, Lex What. I'm Yorrick What." The pair shook hands. "Nice to meet you."

"Likewise," Lex replied.

"You sound smart. You educated?"

Lex looked to the sky. "Not in the traditional sense." Returning to earth, he added, "Same kind of education I assume you have—Streets University."

Yorrick chortled. "What's the job?"

"The guy involved in Igwe Agu's death. We're annihilating him; everyone he knows."

"I thought it was a suicide."

"Well that's not good enough for ol' Nwanneka. He wants the man ruined." Lex scratched his cheek. "We start with his outer ring of friends and move inward. *Carthago delenda est.*"

"What does that mean?"

"It means were going to tear his life to the ground and pour salt on the rubble."

The older man hummed in appreciation of the sentiment. "Where'd you learn that?"

"I read a book once." Lex changed beats like a train at a railroad switch. "Research begins now. Finish your cigar. We're going out of town."

Yorrick stared dully, unsure how to react to being given orders. After a final inhale, he threw down the cigarillo and crushed it under his boot.

~

Yorrick stomped ahead of Lex down the freezer aisle. A case of beers swung by two fingers at his side. He stopped abruptly and jerked open a freezer door; the seal ripped loudly, and the glass fogged. With his free hand, Yorrick seized a box of frozen Buffalo wings and let the door crash.

Next, they set a course for the checkout lines. Yorrick plopped his beer and Buffalo wings onto a conveyor belt, behind which Lex placed his own items: celery and a jug of water. Yorrick scoffed. "You forgot the lipstick, Nancy."

"When you're old and fat, popping Tums like Tic-Tacs, then say something, Yorkie," Lex retorted.

"Don't you dare start calling me that."

The checkout girl swiped and bagged their items. When they finished paying, Yorrick plodded for the exit. His stride was suddenly halted when the foothold of a wheelchair struck his ankle.

"I'm so sorry," said a woman behind the wheelchair wearing a white, wool coat. She smiled at Yorrick, who glared back and gave the wheelchair a kick. The woman stumbled backward, trying to keep the chair steady. The brown sack of groceries sitting in her feeble passenger's lap toppled. Yorrick snorted and tramped out of the store.

In a flash, Lex was at the wheelchair's side, re-bagging their groceries. The woman knelt down to join him.

"Thank you," she said, flustered. "Do you know that guy?"

"Better than I'd like to."

Lex stood with the full bag.

"Dad, are you okay?" the woman asked. The man's entire body shook incessantly. His knees were bulbous between two muscleless leg bones. Pencil-thin neck barely strong enough to support his skull, he laboriously rocked his head in affirmation; two decrepit fingers signaled for the sack.

Lex carefully replaced the groceries. Then, for the first time, he looked at the woman full in the face. His chest became hollow. The last time he'd seen it was at the window of an old Detroit apartment building. He had been so thirsty to kiss her then. The feeling wasn't foreign even now.

She smiled self-consciously. Lex inwardly chided himself for staring.

"Well, thanks again." With a polite finger wave, she resumed pushing her father to the exit. Halfway through the automatic doors the girl stopped and twisted her head around. Lex pretended not to see. Her cool-water eyes scrutinized him intensely. A bleached smile erupted, and she spun forward, standing still only a second longer. Lex restrained himself from following. He was forgetting the one-eyed troll and their job together. He clamped his teeth; she knew the old Lex. He was leaving Detroit anyway.

~

"Hi. This is Kip Swanson. I'm not here, so leave a message."

Oramus waited for the tone. "Hey, Kip. This is Oramus. It's Thursday, about eleven. Just returning your call. You've moved already; that was fast—"

"Hello," a crisp, female voice interrupted. "Seattle Police. I'm sorry to tell you this, but Kip Swanson passed away last night."

"What?" The breath congealed in his throat. "How?"

"I'm sorry; I can't say. Were you a friend of his?"

At length, Oramus answered, "Yes. Yes, I was."

The woman grunted in forced compassion. "Yes. Well, again, I apologize for the bad news. When we have more information, we'll be sure to notify you. What is your name and telephone number?"

"My name's Oramus Krand. My number is 512-472-9495."

"Alright, Mr. Krand. We will contact you as soon as possible."

Oramus' brow was fixed in furrow. He docked the receiver sloppily and sped back to the hospital room.

When he arrived, Gwen was reclining on a massive pillow. She smiled at his entrance. "Did you talk to Kip?" Then, absorbing Oramus' expression, "What's wrong?"

"He's dead."

"What?" Gwen gasped.

"Police answered the phone; said he died yesterday."

~

Nwanneka Agu stared with menacing eyes, hands clutching biceps, at an authoritative Pisani hanging on the wall in a golden frame. The man's unwavering black eyes matched his midnight blazer. Nwanneka's intensity waned when he heard a cough. He rotated to find a frail Asian man wearing a plaid long-sleeve, brown slacks and leather shoes. He carried a large, square item wrapped in newspaper. Nwanneka met the oddity with a look of momentary confusion.

"Hello, Mr. Agu," began the stranger.

"Greetings," replied the black man with a warm, white smile.

"Valletta? Aren't there enough museums in France?" The man's eyebrows peaked from behind his spectacles.

"I have seen them all," Nwanneka said with distaste, "—many times. Maltese pieces are refreshing."

"Yes. Pisani was indeed a master."

"Yes he was. You are familiar with his work?" asked Nwanneka, intrigued.

"Well, yes and no. Not as familiar as you are, I am sure. But I do recall a couple of his works from my studies. The paintings in St. Philip's Parish Church in Zebbug are my favorites."

"You went to a university. I was not as lucky," Nwanneka said with surety.

"Actually, I was tutored. I considered attending a university but couldn't afford one."

"I see. I learned strictly from books I read as a boy in America and later on in France. But we are here to do business, yes? What have you for me?" Nwanneka lifted his great hand as a gesture to commence walking. They strolled abreast in the carpeted hall of the museum.

"First of all, as a token of good will," the Asian man said, offering his tote, "I've brought you a gift."

"My! Good taste and good manners. You are making a good impression." Nwanneka ripped through the layer of newspaper with a fingernail and removed a book, crumpling the gift-wrap with his spare hand. "My God!" he said, slowing the walk nearly to a stop. "The Holy Bible, illustrations by Gustave Doré. Amazing. This is an original copy?"

"It is," the Asian man asserted. "It belonged to my grandfather's French master."

Nwanneka opened the book to an arbitrary page in Genesis and read the title of an illustration. "*The Death of Abel*. These are fascinating, aren't they?"

"Very."

"Doré is one of my favorites, you know." Nwanneka touched his companion's shoulder. "Token accepted. *Merci*."

"On the contrary, thank you for taking the time to meet me."

As they approached a trash receptacle, Nwanneka disposed of the newspaper. "Of course, of course, Doctor—I'm sorry. I know you told me on the phone; what was it?"

"Bonfois."

"Dr. Bonfois. Yes. I apologize. Now what can I do for you?"

"Well, I read about your brother in *The Times*, and you have my deepest condolences."

"Thank you."

Fao-cun swallowed. "I wonder—do you ever suspect it wasn't suicide?"

"I know it wasn't," Nwanneka answered decidedly. "It was Krand. A good friend of mine witnessed it."

"Then I assume—" Fao-cun lowered his voice. "I assume you have someone to *deal* with him?"

"Mhm."

"And what of his son?"

"How do you know Krand has a son?"

"Krand and I have—history. And I have my own score to settle with him."

"I already have plans for the wife and child," Nwanneka answered dispassionately.

"What if I could make you a bargain?" the petite man ventured.

"Which would be . . . ?"

"I am willing to purchase the son's safety."

"You assume I have a price."

"Not at all, Mr. Agu. I understand your need for reprisal, but consider it a plea. All I have to offer for the boy is 200,000 francs."

"Dr. Bonfois, that's at least 25,000 pounds!"

"I know it isn't much to you. I'm only a teacher."

"No, no; it's an attractive offer. I'll put some thought into it."

"I'm glad you can trust me."

"Thank you," Nwanneka laughed, "but it isn't you I trust; it's your background check."

Fao-cun smirked. "Wise."

"Did you have anything else, Doctor?"

"That's all I came to say, Mr. Agu."

Nwanneka waved an arm. "Well, we've not finished browsing. You've proven to be a cultured man. Join me for the afternoon?"

"Thank you, Mr. Agu; I would be honored."

They stood side-by-side, facing a tableau of a countryside blanketed by violet buds.

"I've never seen a landscape I didn't want to step into," Nwanneka whispered.

"That's a strength of Impressionism. So serene. Invokes nostalgia." Fao-cun inhaled deeply. "Are you an artist?"

"A beginner."

"Painting lessons?"

Nwanneka chuckled. "I'm in the middle of a project." He turned away from the exhibit. "Imagine a human—nameless, helpless, demoralized, blank. I give it a name, a purpose. It would be as if I have given it life." Nwanneka paused, letting his theory soak. "My art project is to create man, Dr. Bonfois. It is something painters and sculptors have attempted throughout history—and many have come close. But all of them failed to give their canvas life. That is my mission."

~

Oramus shoved the key into his doorknob. He stepped in, absently eyeing a newspaper unfolded and sloppily strewn across the couch. Staring longer, he noticed a chunk had been ripped out of several pages. He looked at the coffee table. A tall glass, sweating profusely, was filled to the brim. Water swelled to the brink of overflowing. Four white twigs floating at the top were the remnants of ice cubes. Oramus closed the door. The apartment was still.

"You there, babe?" Oramus called. He walked across the living room, swerving around an idle vacuum cleaner. "Babe?" He went straight to the bedroom.

Oramus panned the tidy room, gathering that the cradle was also empty. He strode to the window and peeled back the dainty, white lace. Gwen's parking space was vacant. Oramus heaved a sigh, walking backward and crashing on the bed. She must have been at the drug store. The ballooning of his chest became more discrete. Oramus' stomach moaned. He sat up, rubbing his eyes. His stomach complained once more. Oramus stood and ambled to the kitchen.

~

Gwen awoke from the anesthesia in a helicopter. She was flying over vast tundra as far as she could see in all directions. The pilot landed at a remote place that, on the surface, looked hardly different than any other piece of land they had flown over. He hopped out, walked to the cabin and pulled Gwen into the snow by her neck. Freezing wind bombarded her coatless body and whirling snow stung her eyes. She wasn't too cold, for the anesthetic hadn't worn off completely. The pilot clasped her arm and trudged toward what looked like the top of a submerged tank. He hastily kicked the object and withdrew his foot at once.

"*Salop!*" he muttered before stomping the object more carefully. Then they waited. Gwen looked ahead at the horizon, where white earth met white sky. Suddenly, a trap door opened out of the boulder, revealing a bearded blonde. The pilot slapped a palm over Gwen's crown and guided her down a steep staircase to a catwalk lined with cells. Below industrial, armored lamps, the room looked grossly yellow, the color of unkempt teeth, in contrast to the white world above. The pink-faced blonde man held the door of an open cell at the end of the aisle. He wore a fluffy, old parka that had formerly been a tan color but was now soiled and brown. He fit the profile of a Northern European: straight, yellow hair, sparkling, blue eyes, red nose and pink lips. Cheeks like two glossy plums, he smiled, showing teeth almost as white as the snow on the roof.

Gwen glared at him from under her mangled hair.

"Welcome to the warmest little cold place on earth," he said in an overtly Midwestern accent. The pilot ushered Gwen to the cell and shoved her to the hard floor inside. Blondie closed and locked the door, eyes glued to the departing pilot.

"Still won't tell me your name, eh?" he ventured.

The pilot ignored him.

"Alright then. S'long, Johnny!" he burst.

Gwen heard the wind's intensity one last time as the pilot left the enclosure. She crawled to a back corner of her cell and huddled into a ball. Scratching her hand, she realized she could barely feel the fingernails scraping against her skin. Her teeth began to chatter.

"It's about time you started shivering," said Blondie. His pristine voice cracked the silence. "I was beginning to worry." He walked through a doorway at the end of the catwalk into a room beyond Gwen's sight. He returned shortly with another parka, which he finagled through the bars of her cell and let plop onto the floor. "Happens to a lot of folks that come in here. Too mad to feel the cold. Too mad or too afraid."

Gwen was reluctant to retrieve the coat. When Blondie stepped back, she lurched at it like an insect and dragged it to the back of the cell with her foot.

Hiding beneath her new parka, Gwen scanned the prison. She counted five cells on either side of the catwalk where Blondie strolled. Only two others were occupied. Both inmates stared at her like she was a zoo-animal. However, they kept quiet, sensing it too early for salutations. One was a woman, two cells down from Gwen, cloaked sinisterly under a mantle of gray hair. She looked as if she hadn't seen a comb in years. Gwen placed her between fifty and sixty. Wrapped in myriad blankets, the woman crouched like a gargoyle. Her ghostly, yellow eyes watched. Gwen couldn't bring herself to meet them for longer than a fleeting look.

Across the catwalk from the woman reclined a scruffy man with high cheekbones, olive skin and a jagged haircut. Bathing must have been uncommon here. Through an open parka, she glimpsed a black shirt clinging to a well-carved chest. The inmate scraped his teeth incessantly with a long, ugly thumbnail. He wiped the residue on a grungy pair of camo pants. His other hand repeatedly zipped and unzipped a pocket of his parka. His spying eyes seemed permanently half-shut.

"You don't have to say anything. I'll talk." Blondie perched his forehead between two bars of Gwen's cell, wearing a childlike grin. "My name is Ambrose." He pointed to the wild woman. "This beauty to your left is Dolores. She's been here longer than I have."

Dolores muttered a frail greeting not unlike a meow.

"How long has it been, Dolores? Ten years?"

She shrugged.

"She was the first here in Segeltuch." Ambrose gestured to the other inmate. "And this strapping steed is—" The inmate coughed.

"Emmerich," he boomed in a chilling Scottish brogue.

"Emmerich's only been here a couple of months now," Ambrose continued.

"Too damn long," piped Emmerich.

Ambrose lowered his voice almost to a whisper, speaking to Gwen alone. "He doesn't mean that. It's actually quite pleasant here. We'll become best friends, the four of us. Just you wait."

"Pleasant? Here?" Emmerich interrupted. "Why don't you tell her exactly where here is? Give her the speech you gave me."

"I'm getting to that," Ambrose insisted. "Sorry. He's not always this rude." The warden posed before an invisible lectern. "You are in a private penitentiary in the subterrain of Antarctica. As I'm sure you've noticed, there are only ten cells. That's because this prison is not affiliated with any government; no criminals here. This prison is for those who never existed." Ambrose pointed to the new arrival. "That includes you, Miss. You're not real. None of us are. Emmerich, here, he was never born. And as for Dolores, well, you get the picture. This is Segeltuch, and that's what happens while you're here; you're forgotten. Of course, it doesn't happen overnight." He pointed to the ring on Gwen's left hand. "He's missing you very much right now. But in a few years (it won't take long), a few years of the entire world telling him that you were just a very vivid dream, he'll begin to believe it himself. But that's all very gloomy. I like to look at it this way. If you never lived to begin with, you can't very well die, can you? No, Miss. You're immortal." Ambrose looked back at Emmerich. "How was that?"

"Not as good as I remembered. I guess it's a first-time-only thing."

"Must be." Ambrose clapped his hands together. "Alright! Who's ready to party?"

"Party? What party?" demanded Emmerich.

"The welcoming party." Ambrose darted into the unseen chamber.

Emmerich called after him, "We never had a welcoming party for me!"

Gwen heard the clinking of glass bottles and other rustling. Ambrose returned shortly holding a bottle of wine and four glasses. Wine sloshed in the half-empty bottle. He stopped first at Dolores' cage and poured the old woman a glass, passing it to her between the bars. She drank in gulps. Ambrose did the same for Emmerich, who savored. He released a raucous bellow. "Christ, that's delicious. Then again, you probably could've poured a glass of piss, and I'd be satisfied."

"I'll remember that," Ambrose answered, pouring a dab of wine for himself. Finally, he placed the remaining glass and bottle on the floor of Gwen's cell. "You can finish it off," he said with a smile. Once his back was turned, Gwen lunged forward and shattered them against the bars of her cell with a hard kick. A few ruby droplets speckled the calves of Ambrose' insulated pants. In a blink, Gwen was back to cowering in the corner. Ambrose studied her, swishing a draft about in his mouth. Wine dripped slowly and lamentably from the cell bars. Setting his glass on the catwalk, he seized a saffron block and a jack-knife from his pockets. As he peeled away the first petal of cellophane, the eye-watering stench of aged cheese diffused across the room. Putting the jack-knife to work, he tossed a hunk to Dolores, which she devoured whole. Ambrose chuckled and threw a second piece to Emmerich, who caught it in his free hand and sniffed.

"Och, that's rank. Cheddar?" he asked.

"The one and only," Ambrose replied, chomping down the yellow slab.

"Well, normally I'd prefer goat cheese."

"I'm a Wisconsiner." Ambrose grinned, showing globs of cheese in his teeth. He re-wrapped the block and rolled it into Gwen's cell; she sneered. Ambrose squatted to the balls of his feet. His eyes dared her to throw it back.

Gwen hid behind her knees.

"Better eat it, kiddo. They don't send us a lot of food." He paused. "We get a shipment of new clothes every six months—burn the laundry. You can bathe as often as you like; I'll boil up some hot water, but it turns cold real quick." Ambrose stood to his full height. "Oh, and Emmerich gets to see you naked."

"That's droll!" Emmerich blasted. "I won't look."

The facility quieted as Ambrose took to a stool to finish his wine.

"Hey, Brosey," piped Emmerich, "I've been thinking. We're in Antarctica, right? So this facility is basically dug out of a continental sheet of ice."

"Something like that."

After pausing to suck a bite of cheese, Emmerich continued. "Am I crazy, or could a number of things go wrong here? The ice melts, and then what happens to us?"

Ambrose sat back with a humored expression.

"Either the prison floods, and we all drown, or we sink down to the seabed to suffocate—if the water pressure doesn't crush us like a trash compactor. Then you have to consider the ice shifting or breaking. If the ice separates, again we fall to our imminent death. But if it pushes together, we're jam."

Brows crested, Ambrose chirped, "Exciting!"

Emmerich smacked noisily. "You know how Antarctica's shaped like a rubber ducky?"

"Mhm."

"About where are we on the duck?"

"Square on the ass."

"Well that's downright poetic," Emmerich grumbled. "So I've heard your speech twice now, and something's bugging me. If they wanted to erase us, why not just feed us to the fishes? Consider the expenses of keeping us alive. It doesn't make sense."

"Otherwise they would have no reason to hire me," Ambrose jested. "The owner wants you for a personal project. That's all I know. And you're not the only ones. There's a sister facility somewhere called Mokra Glina."

"These names. What does Segeltuch mean anyway?"

Ambrose shrugged. "I didn't name it."

A voice croaked from Gwen's cell. "It's German for 'canvas'." The newcomer suddenly commanded all eyes in the room.

~

An indefinite time later, Ambrose shut off the lights from a breaker behind the steps. The jail fell black. Then the crying began. As hysteria commandeered, hours flowed further into what may have been the night. Gwen's sobs cycled between wails and whines.

At some point, Dolores howled, "Shut up!"

"You shut up!" countered the Scot.

Fits of adrenaline caused Gwen to bash her skull repeatedly against the unbudging floor. She clawed with serrated fingernails.

~

Gwen awoke facedown, cheek to the ground, bruised and exhausted. The lights were on; she stirred.

Ambrose' voice broke the crisp air. "Side-effects may include despair, rage, terror, yearning and self-mutilation. Some take it harder than others." Gwen remained still as possible, hoping he would leave her alone. "Tonight will not be so long. I promise."

She lay motionless for a few moments but sensed Ambrose' eyes watching her all the while. He knew she was awake. Gwen lifted her head to survey the room. Dolores sat cross-legged and drooping, while Emmerich shaved with a straight razor that must have belonged to Ambrose. The warden sat on a stool right outside Gwen's cell. She scooted back to her wall, pulling away loose strands of hair that still clung to her damp cheeks. A groan bubbled from her belly. The block of cheddar by her feet began to call. Gwen snatched it up and quickly shed the cellophane. The corners of the cheese were stale and hard. With a jagged thumbnail, she shaved off white and blue-green splotches that plagued its surface. Finally, she severed a piece onto her tongue, using as few teeth as possible.

"I heard Dolores had a rather insensitive streak last night," Ambrose asserted. Gwen looked at the old woman, abashed.

In the tiniest voice, Dolores muttered, "Sorry."

"Good," Ambrose interjected. "No harm done. So tell us about yourself, Miss. What's your name?"

Gwen's lips remained cemented together.

"Not yet? Okay." He shrugged and quietly moved into the unseen room.

The cheese disappeared, Emmerich finished shaving, and Dolores curled up for a nap. Gwen stared at her shoes, realizing with some dread that most of the days in her future would probably take this turn. As she settled in on the back wall of her cell, a faint sound wriggled into her ears. She concentrated, straining to verify the sound's existence. Finally, she snapped her head up to find the source, and her eyes lit upon Emmerich. He was singing.

> *I've loved thee, Old Scotia, and love thee I will,*
> *'til the heart that now beats in by bosom is still.*
> *My forefathers loved thee, for often they drew their dirks in defense of thy banners of blue;*
> *though murky thy glens, where the wolf prowled of yore, and craggy thy mountains, where cataracts roar,*
> *the race of old Albyn, when danger was nigh, for thee stood resolved still to conquer or die.*

As Emmerich continued chanting softly to himself, Gwen's mind began to wander. She thought first of her husband. Gwen clenched her teeth and began to cry as undisturbingly as she could. She remembered something Oramus had said not long before they married.

~

The pair stood on a Dallas city sidewalk under artificial lights and smog. They had just seen a show at the Inwood and were loitering outside of the theatre. Oramus grasped Gwen's fingers with his right hand and balled his left into a fist.

"They say the human heart is about the size of a fist. Less than a pound in weight." He met her eyes with an arresting gaze. "There may be times in your life when you lose everything, when you don't have a penny to your name, nothing to lay claim to. But you should know that you will always have at least this much." Oramus laid his fist into Gwen's palm and closed her fingers around it. "Less than a pound in weight."

~

Gwen bit hard into the sleeve of her parka. Her whole body pulsed in muted sobbing.

Now Gwen met the image of her baby. Talbot Fitch Krand had been born only two months ago.

~

Fao-cun reclined in the driver's seat of a rental sedan, shirt unbuttoned and hair in cowlicks. Empty water bottles littered the floorboards. Five floors of Austin apartments rose up before him. Their doors opened onto railed balconies, bounded on each side by open stairwells. His eyelids sagged, having kept a thirty-eight-hour watch already. In his lap, he cradled a small, black-and-silver camera. He reached into the passenger seat for a jar of nuts. It was his second-to-last, sharing the seat with a plastic bag of five or six apples and a small cluster of bananas. He opened the jar and shook some nuts into his hand. Peanuts mostly and a few almonds; one pecan; no luck with cashews. He tossed them back like pills, crunching loudly, and replaced the container.

Fao-cun leaned forward, retraining his gaze—third tier, fourth door from the right. Gwen had taken the trash out four hours ago, but remained in since. Fao-cun had expected Nwanneka's "special plans" for her to have begun by now; he was sweating patience. Only insurance on a 25,000-pound transaction kept his endurance alive.

A delivery truck arrived on the lot. Fao-cun froze like a deer in watch. Parking near the rightmost stairwell, a man stepped down from the cab in coveralls, sunglasses and a cap. He threw open the back, lowered a ramp and rolled out a large, wooden box on a dolly. After wheeling his freight to the stairwell, he slowly climbed to the third stage. Fao-cun's eyes followed like magnets as the driver passed the first door, then the second, then third. The dolly came to a careful halt in front of the fourth door—Gwen's door. Removing an item from his pocket, the driver huddled over the doorknob. The door suddenly swung inward, and the man promptly invaded with his carriage, systematically shutting the door after him.

Fao-cun remained staring, breathless, at the closed door. He could hardly believe what he was witnessing. The door reopened in minutes; Fao-cun's focus hadn't abandoned it once. The driver left, whistling a tune and pushing the same wooden box before him, which now rolled with more languor. Fao-cun snapped his camera up to one eye and set on the shutter button like a madman. Through the viewfinder, he noticed a hook-shaped scar behind the driver's right ear. He zoomed in on the mark and continued photographing wildly.

~

"Delphin Soignet. He's an intelligence operative. DGSE."

"Really," Fao-cun blurted into the receiver.

"You're lucky he had the scar," answered a mature, British voice. "Database found him right off. Otherwise, I don't know; his face is hard to make out in the pictures."

"Sorry. I'm not a photographer."

"What are you into, Fao-cun, asking me about this guy?"

"Nothing serious. But I'd rather keep it to myself."

"Of course," the man replied, deadpan.

"Do you know where I can find him?"

"He lives in Paris. Seventeen Rue Main Gauche, Apartment Four."

Fao-cun repeated as he copied the address.

"Listen. Whatever you're doing, be careful."

"Thanks, Tanner. And thanks for your help. I owe you."

"Just don't make it a habit. I do try to break the law as little as possible."

"What would the Yard do without you?"

"Pay my pension," the man chuckled huskily.

~

Fao-cun calmly knocked on the door and clasped his hands in front of him. Almost immediately, the door swished open, showing a man in his thirties with dark, parted hair and a black turtleneck.

"*Désolé de vous déranger,*" Fao-cun began quickly, "*mais je voudrais vous poser quelques questions.*"

"*Qui êtes-vous?*" the resident spat in a bass timbre.

Fao-cun leaned in, speaking low. "*Quelqu'un qui sait ce que vous faites.*"

For some seconds, the man squinted, searching Fao-cun's eyes. He looked back over his left shoulder, exposing a scar behind his ear. With a final huff, he stepped to one side. "*Entrez.*"

Fao-cun strode inside, soles clunking on the somber, wood floor. The apartment smelled of lemon soap. Fao-cun immediately noticed how meticulously the room was organized: all the furniture squarely placed; magazines stacked and aligned in the corner of a coffee table; the hanging print of Dobell's *Wangi Boy* could balance a marble. The room felt spacious, its barebones arrangement lacking any surplus.

Fao-cun brushed a hand over his thin, combed hair as his host shut the door. The Frenchman gestured to a three-piece sitting area to their left. "*Asseyez-vous.*"

"*Merci.*" Fao-cun sank into a rigid, wooden chair next to a matching sidetable.

The host sat on a low futon across from him. He scratched his cheek plagued by five o'clock shadow; it crackled like sandpaper. His pale, thick lips began to protrude. "*Donc—*"

"*Peut-on parler en anglais, s'il vous plaît?*" Fao-cun interrupted.

"If you wish. Your French is no good?"

"It's fine. I'd just feel more comfortable if we spoke English."

"By all means then."

Fao-cun took a deep, shaky breath. "The woman you kidnapped in Austin—"

The Frenchman broke into laughter.

"—what did you do with her?"

"You really do know something. And so direct!"

Fao-cun waited, brow tense with unease, for the host's mirth to fade.

The Frenchman sighed, and his face settled into a look of annoyance, amazement and commiseration, baring all three at once like a prism in sunlight. Finally, he answered, "She is locked away in Antarctica; I flew her there myself. In Wilkes Land, if you want to know."

Fao-cun blinked vacuously at the Frenchman's candor.

"Now," the host continued. "There is a pistol taped under your seat. Would you hand it to me, please?"

~

Nwanneka skimmed mindlessly through a stack of letters and packages on his desk, tossing some here, others there. Suddenly, he paused. He dropped them all, save for the one under his thumb. It was blank; no stamps or addresses. He flipped it over. Nothing. Holding the envelope up to a light, Nwanneka confirmed that it was indeed a letter. His hand dove into a desk-drawer for a bejeweled paper knife, fluidly slicing through the seal. He extracted the letter with care, unfolded it and began reading:

Monsieur Agu,

Vous recevrez peut-être bientôt des nouvelles de ma mort dans les avis de décès. Je vous prie de ne surtout pas vous inquiéter. Afin de protéger mon identité, j'ai été forcé de feindre le suicide. Ne vous ennuyez pas avec les bagatelles. Je réglerai les derniers détails. Je reste, cependant, votre fidèle serviteur. En vous remerciant de la confiance que vous me témoignez, je vous prie d'accepter, Monsieur Agu, l'expression de mes respectueux hommages.

Delphin Soignet

Mr. Agu,

You may soon receive news of my obituary. Please do not be alarmed. In order to protect my identity, I have been forced to feign suicide. Do not bother yourself with the details. All loose ends will be adequately tied up. I remain, however, your faithful employee.

Respect,
Delphin Soignet

Twenty elapsed years

Oramus scraped the bottom of the little, cardboard cup and spooned into his mouth the last dab of melted mocha ice cream. Pastels plagued the petite ice cream parlor, where Oramus sat alone. He was constantly aware of the spying scooper, longhaired and lanky. His cup came to rest on the table with a small, hollow thud. As Oramus sat idly, whiffing the aroma of fresh-baked waffle cones, a hand steadily drifted to his shirt pocket and extracted a bright green marble. He hefted the token and rolled it around his palm before burying the marble tightly in his fist. Next, Oramus met his faint reflection in the glass table. His dark brown hair was shaved to a thin film over a red scalp. His bronze, leathery face was beginning to wrinkle. The corners of his mouth hung in flaps around his chin, giving him the look of a permanent frown. A scar ran from his forehead, down the temple and stopped at his cheekbone. Oramus unclenched the marble and held it over his eye so as to cover his iris in the reflection. Finally, he rolled the marble in his palm once more before returning it to his pocket.

Oramus' wallet became thick under his weight. He tried to shift, but the bulging wallet would not deflate. Oramus removed the brown leather wallet and plopped it onto the table, where it fell open. Oramus spread apart its edges.

Wedged between a five, three ones, a recital ticket and a deli receipt, lay an infant's sock—the only proof of his son's existence; it was all he had left. Oramus' mind floated like an alabaster cloud to his wife's thin fingers slow-dancing on the keys of a grand piano, graceful as piece from *Swan Lake.* She played wordless lullabies, while Oramus watched from over the piano lid. The notes haunted him now. He hastily tucked the sock back into his wallet.

~

Rick heard a slapping at his screen. He moseyed to the door, working to keep up with the wooden cane under his red palm. Rick opened his front door and looked grumpily at a middle-aged visitor in a short-sleeve button-down, cargo shorts and sneakers. The man had a defined scar on the upper side of his face.

"Can I help y'?" asked the man in his late seventies.

"I'm Oramus Krand."

The old man's blue eyes blossomed under gray eyebrows. "Hell." He shifted his weight and nudged the cowboy hat off his forehead. "Get in here." Rick turned and began to wobble toward the kitchen.

Oramus pulled open the screen door and stepped inside.

"Have a seat," Rick said. "Anywhere but the recliner."

"'Kay." Oramus looked around the old, familiar living room. Most of the racing trophies were gone. Numerous African game heads had replaced them. Oramus recognized one to be a gemsbok and one, the prize hanging above the mantle, a cape buffalo. The smells were the same. Rick must have still chewed. Sitting on a red area rug were Rick's recliner and a sunken couch. Both faced a dusty, oval coffee table. Moving a pillow, Oramus took a seat on the sofa. He laid the pillow on his lap, squeezing the edges like a stress ball. Bumping glass chimed from the kitchen; cabinets opened and closed. "Can I give you a hand in there?"

"Nope. I'm fixin' drinks. What'll y' have?"

"Do you have any pure grain?"

Rick chuckled. "Try again." His voice had grown hoarser in his old age.

"Then how 'bout a German Schnaps?"

"You got it. Think I'll have one, too."

More glass-clinking filled the silence.

Oramus wanted to make conversation. "What's with the heads?"

"Hmm? Oh." The elder paused to collect his thoughts. "Later in life, I got into African big-game hunting. Me and Raz went on a few hunts together; it's been several years now." Rick chuckled. "God, I loved it! Never done it before. I'll tell y' some stories in a little while."

"I'd love to hear them." Oramus observed a figurine sitting on the coffee table. It depicted a male lion pouncing through tall grass onto a batch of cubs gathered to play. The beast's arms were outstretched like wings, claws bared like daggers. He hung, frozen, above the defenseless cubs, ready to come to life and pummel them at any moment. Oramus felt slightly unnerved. However, something else seemed strange. It wasn't a simple ceramic knick-knack. The lion's mane was clearly textile, nylon perhaps.

"Ain't that something?" Rick dropped two squat glasses onto the table, causing a small splash. Then he fell backward into his recliner, laid the cane across his lap and placed his hat on a sidetable. "I bought that in South Africa. Every last hair in that mane is from a real lion hide." He nodded, admiring the find. "You know, those dominant males actually do that sometimes—kill the cubs. Fascinatin', I think. Sad—but fascinatin' all the same."

Oramus nodded, coming out of a daze. He saw Rick perched in the chair like a sock monkey. He was much skinnier now, wearing extra-large, blue coveralls. His head, roofed in soft, fine silver, leaned gently onto one shoulder. Oramus found his eyes, and they shared a quiet smile.

"Alright," Rick said, "shoot."

Oramus knew exactly what he meant. "Well," he sighed, reaching for the Schnaps. Rick noted that whatever British twang ever existed in Oramus' voice had now completely diluted. "You remember my wife?"

"Yeah." Rick thought for a moment. "Dodge Alby's little girl."

Oramus nodded. He swirled the clear beverage in his glass. "I came home from work one day, and she wasn't there. Neither was the baby. Her car was gone, so I figured she was out. A few hours passed; still no sign of her. I tried calling some friends to see if anyone knew where she was—no one. When I called the police, they told me to wait until morning. I waited, but she never came back."

"Did they find her?"

Oramus shook his head.

"Why didn't I hear about this on the news?"

Oramus began to talk faster, as if he was finally getting to something he had been trying to say. "There was something else I noticed that day. All of our pictures—the framed ones around the house and all our photo albums—they were all gone. And all the drawers in our desk were empty."

The gaze from Rick's beady pupils could have bored through steel.

"I check our records. Their birth certificates, social security cards, our marriage certificate—gone. Her wallet was gone, so no driver's license either. So I started looking for handwriting samples: signatures, letters, journals, textbooks. Nothing. Police dusted the apartment; no fingerprints. They even dusted her car, which was missing its plates, registration, and proof of insurance." Oramus' eyes were watering. "I went back to her parents' houses for baby pictures, yearbooks, things like that, but both of them had moved. The neighbors didn't know where." Oramus choked. "It was like, suddenly, everything that had to do with her just vanished." The glaze on his eyes began to drip. "It wasn't on the news, because the police didn't think she existed," Oramus laughed feebly.

The men finished their spirits without words, while Oramus regained his composure.

"Where'd y' go after that?" Rick finally resumed.

"I wandered around for a while, confused. After it really hit me a second time that my family was gone, I decided to get away. I didn't want to have anything to do with my old life. I quit racing; sold everything; stopped writing my foster-father; stopped sending you payments. I apologize for that, by the way."

"Don't worry about that. I had plenty to keep me going."

Oramus leaned to one side, reaching into his back pocket. He pulled out a large, stuffed envelope and dropped it on the coffee table. "Still, this belongs to you. It's the rest of the payments on the car, the pit crew, the lessons and everything else. All in large bills."

"Thank you, son. Is that what y' came here for?"

Oramus nodded.

"Well alright then." Rick took a slow breath. "Go on. Y' sold everything; then what?"

"I got a job off-shore. Oil rig. Kept it ever since. I'm on break right now. Go back in two weeks."

"Where are y' staying? Y're welcome to stay here."

Oramus raised his hand in refusal. "I'm at a motel in Austin."

~

Sitting on the end of a fusty, maroon motel bed, back straight, hands on knees, Oramus mentally replayed his conversation with Rick that afternoon. Now alone again, he was in awe at how much he had said. By his account, it was the most he had ever spoken of the ordeal with anyone. Oramus had intended to drop off his last payment and go, answering any questions as briefly as possible. Somehow that didn't happen.

A knock sounded at the door. Oramus hurriedly stepped over his open suitcase and answered. The security chain stopped the door at a fist-width. A visitor with salt-and-pepper hair almost as short as Oramus' smiled in.

"Hello?" Oramus shot.

"Brother, you are about the hardest man I've ever had to track down," the man greeted. His green eyes shone like jade stones.

Oramus' face drained to wraithlike pallor. "Lex?"

"Can I come in?"

Oramus unlatched the door and flung it open. He stood awkwardly in the doorway, unsure of the next move. Lex embraced him.

"Surprised?"

"Yeah," Oramus admitted. "How'd you find me here?"

"After learning you had no permanent residence, I got knee-deep in some research and discovered you work off-shore. So I talked to your foreman who told me you came here for a couple weeks. Then I drove to Austin, found a phonebook and checked every hotel until I got the right one: Mo'Rest Motel. Interesting choice."

"Can I take your coat?" Oramus offered.

Lex clutched the chest of his jacket. "No, thanks. I'll keep it on."

Oramus indicated a chair by the bed. "Have a seat?"

"Sure," Lex responded.

Oramus kicked his suitcase out of the way with an apology. He sat on the edge of the bed, facing Lex. "Where do we begin?" he embarked.

"I guess where we left off."

"Well." Oramus faltered. "Well, what'd you do with your life, Lex?"

"I joined the Navy."

"Did you go to school?"

"I got a G.E.D."

Oramus tensed as an icy hand clutched the windpipe in his chest. "Look, Lex, I'm sorry for leaving you in Detroit—"

"Don't," shot Lex. "I've turned out well enough. I live in Colorado. Got a small business and a woman who loves me. Her name's Piche. I'm doing all right." Lex slapped his brother's knee. "But you. What are you doing on an oil rig? I wouldn't have figured you for a roughneck. You a geologist or something?"

"Nope. Drilling crew. I like the job because it pays well; I don't have to pay a mortgage; and I get to be alone for the most part."

The brothers stared at one another.

"Are we just catching up, or did you come here to say something?" Oramus inquired.

At length, Lex replied, "Both. Foremost, I wanted to catch up, but I guess that'll have to wait."

"Is this something I won't want to hear?"

Lex nodded wearily. Silence drew on.

"Well?" Oramus asked.

"All the shit that happened to you—it wasn't just bad luck. It was Jungle Tears."

"I'm not stupid, Lex. I guessed that much in twenty years."

"After you killed Igwe, Tears hired an assassin to pick off your friends and relatives."

"Yorrick Eberley," Oramus declared. "He killed Kip Swanson."

"He pulled the trigger"—Lex fixed his emeralds on Oramus—"but I was the assassin."

~

Lex tasted iron on his lips. In the umbral night, a black door stared him dead in the face. Lex awaited the muffled shatter. There it was, tailed by a thud. *Klutz*, he thought. Furious footsteps ensued. Lex heard a crack of wood, then two gunshots. Silence. Seconds later, the door bolt clacked. A frazzled-looking Yorrick opened the door, still gripping his silvery revolver, his other hand wrapped in a bath towel. Breathing heavily, he pointed his handgun at a body lying atop a splintered coffee table. Chess pieces lay strewn about the afroed corpse, who stared absently at the ceiling. He pointed a 10-gauge shotgun toward a glassless window. Lex stepped inside the dim apartment.

"Sounded good. How'd it go?"

"I hid beside that hallway and buffaloed him in the back of the head soon as he came out. He fell onto the coffee table, and I shot twice. Nailed him in the chest," Yorrick boasted.

"Once," the youth corrected. "Looks like one of them hit the couch."

Yorrick cast him a scowl.

Lex pulled on a pair of latex gloves and knelt beside the body. "Did anyone see you?"

"Nope."

"Why don't you go to the window, and make sure?"

"Hey!" Yorrick roared, taking a step toward Lex. "We're partners, remember? I do the deed. You do the clean up. Don't bother getting bossy."

"You don't want to get caught any more than I do. Just check the window."

Yorrick pouted to the drafty opening, tramping across glass shards. He brushed off the windowsill with his towel and peered down to the lifeless parking lot below. All lights in surrounding buildings were snuffed.

"Hey, Yorkie," said Lex.

"What?" Yorrick turned around. In an instant, a wave of lead pellets shredded through his chest and ejected a shower of blood onto the wall behind him. The impact of the buckshot hammered Yorrick against the wall, smearing his own blood like a large paintbrush. He toppled into a heap of bleeding rag doll on the carpet.

Lex softly laid the shotgun back down on the floor with Kip's cold finger still clutching the trigger. He stood and sneered at Yorrick's diced flesh. Then, suspecting the police might already be on their way, Lex bolted the door and dipped through the toothy window.

~

Deep trenches had set in Oramus' brow; he gaped at the floor, petrified.

"Wait before you think badly of me."

"Lex, you—murdered my friend."

The felon unzipped his jacket and removed an orange, clasped envelope. "Read this," he commanded, handing the file to his brother.

Oramus accepted the envelope and removed its contents. Beneath a large picture of Kip, a single slip of paper read: *Uche Agu; a.k.a. Kip Swanson, United States; a.k.a. Yul Valagaratz, Luxembourg.*

"This man—your friend—started it all. This man founded the organization that ripped us apart, murdered our father and abducted your wife and son. All of it is his fault. Who knows how many other men's lives he's ruined? He deserved what I gave him."

Oramus remained choked up for many dead, dragging seconds. Finally, he said, "Okay. I just have one question. You knew all of this"—he hefted the envelope—"before you killed Kip, right?"

"Of course. Oramus, I wanted revenge. On everyone who pissed on our lives. And I got two in one night."

Oramus nodded reluctantly.

Lex chuckled. "My motto back then was *Carthago delenda est.* It's an ancient Roman political slogan from the Punic Wars. 'Carthage must be destroyed.' Jungle Tears was my Carthage. And I was Hannibal."

Oramus squinted, still working through the details. "So Jungle Tears hired you to kill its founder?"

"Evidently, when they told me to kill your friends, they didn't realize that included Uche."

"Why'd you wait for the order?"

"I had intended to wait longer, but when opportunity knocks."

"How'd you know it was Kip?"

"It was at one of your races—"

"You went to my races?" Oramus blurted.

"Just a couple," Lex confessed.

"Why didn't you—?"

"You'd just gotten married; you were starting a real life. I didn't want to interrupt."

Oramus' throat tightened as he tried to squeeze out words.

Lex resumed. "It was the Cleveland race—the one the Argentinean took home. I was sitting kind of high on the bleachers, and I spotted someone in the crowd. It was Igwe Agu's head goon, Asp Louche—dressed in a slightly less flamboyant get-up than usual," he added with a smirk, "but I knew it was him."

~

Asp shuffled down the long, flat stairs of the stadium, cradling a paper boat of nachos and sweeping a cane over the ground at his feet. Face forward, he cut his eyes from side to side behind dark sunglasses. Spectators watched him, unafraid of being noticed. Carefully, Asp descended stair-by-stair until he reached his row. He ran his fingertips along grooves in the cold, aluminum bench, until they touched the burgundy, leather fedora he had left to save his place. Plopping the hat atop his shell of taut hair, he sank to the bench and placed the cane at his feet. Finally, Asp attacked the weighty mound of nachos, watchful not to get cheese on his gold ring.

When he had finished gorging on the soggy Tex-Mex, Asp laid the empty boat beside him on the bleacher, noisily sucking his fingers clean. He removed a pen from inside his blazer and smoothed out a napkin over his thigh. *To Aspen and Cassie,* he traced, *who just turned 13 and 10.* Asp glimpsed from the corner of his eye a young boy bounding down the stadium stairs. He swiftly shot an arm into the aisle, halting the boy midstep. Without uttering a word, the child gazed sheepishly at the smiling man in opaque glasses.

"Young man, how old are you?" Asp inquired.

"Nine," he peeped.

"Nine!" Asp gasped. "You sound at least fifteen!"

The boy grinned.

"Now, what do you say to earning five bucks from a blind man?"

"Okay."

"You see, I promised my two little nieces I'd get Rudy Vincenz's autograph for them, but it's hard for me to get around down there. Think you could help me out?"

"Sure."

"Good deal! Well, I'll go ahead and pay you in advance 'cause I trust you." Asp fished a five-dollar bill out of his wallet and enclosed it in the child's fist. "What's your name?" he asked.

"Daniel."

"Daniel. Strong name." He slapped the boy's shoulder firmly. "Pleasure to meet you." Asp beamed. Handing Daniel the napkin, he added, "Just ask him to sign this, and bring it back to me, alright?"

"Okay."

"Thank you, Daniel."

"You're welcome."

"Now hurry, before the race starts!" He nudged Daniel down the stairs.

As the boy scuttled off to Vincenz's station, Asp's warm smile melted away. Wedging the cane beneath his arm, he zipped downstairs to the stadium exit. His message was sent. *To Aspen and Cassie, who just turned 13 and 10.* He would soon meet Rudy Vincenz at 1310 Cass Avenue.

~

Lex scratched his cheek. "The whole blind gag set me on alert right away. Then when he left before the race even started, after coming all the way to Cleveland, I knew something was happening. I watched the kid go up to Rudy Vincenz, and it clicked. That was the moment I realized Rudy Vincenz was in business with Igwe Agu."

"And Kip?" Oramus shook his head, blinking. "I mean Uche?"

Lex paused to organize his thoughts. "Well, from the beginning I figured Uche would be somewhere inconspicuous, but close enough to keep an eye on business. After the Vincenz thing dawned on me, I noticed his pit captain fit the profile. At first I shrugged it off, but as the race went on, I thought about it more and more." Lex's voice slowed to molasses. "I mean, it did make sense. By the end, I had to know, so I improvised a little test."

~

Kip stood, arms crossed, before the seven other members of his crew. They stared soberly at him like pups held in suspense by rubber ball. Some leaned against a cargo trailer, while the rest sat on stacked or upright tires.

"Well, guys," Kip began, rubbing his palms together, "let's pack it up. I'll go try to talk Rudy down."

A gangly, pony-tailed man stood up from his tire, flipping a windshield squeegee in his hand. "There was a time when third place meant beer and strippers all around."

"I don't think third place is what's eating him, Pogo," Kip answered.

A hulk leaning against the trailer chimed in, "I think it's losing to the rookie." His bowling ball head glinted in the early-afternoon sunrays.

A younger crewman reclined in the hole of a tire, fingers laced behind his head. His azure eyes shone vibrantly from the base of a charcoal beanie, behind vintage, horn-rimmed glasses. "Aren't you friends with that guy, Kipster?"

"Yeah," the captain chirped. "Now load up the trailer. Hopefully our driver hasn't thrown a tantrum in the catering tent yet."

As Kip walked away, the youth called after him. "Hey, can you bring us back some of those little smokies? If there are any left!"

Kip laughed over his shoulder and continued the trudge to the food pavilion. Workers still buzzed all around, rolling tires, carrying air wrenches, taking down tents and folding up chairs.

A pedestrian suddenly barreled through Kip's shoulder from behind. "Things fall apart," he growled without braking. Kip stared, thunderstruck, at the fleeting assailant's back, a skull of fine, black hair bobbing like a piston. Kip tore after him.

"Hey!"

The man maintained his brisk march.

"Hey, man!" Kip focused on moving his legs faster. In seconds, he was upon the attacker. He reached out for the hood of the green windbreaker, but the stranger spun on his heels like a mongoose, thrusting his shoulder into Kip's diaphragm. A formidable shove launched the pit captain onto his back. He smacked the gritty earth, fish-like. Empty sky suddenly engulfed his vision. The impact left him wheezing like a bulldog. He winced at the burn of his continually stretching lungs; another wisp of air, and they would pop. By the time Kip could roll onto an elbow, the man had bolted and was scaling a high wall into the stands. He disappeared as vaporously as he had come.

~

"I figured a little Nigerian literature would incite a reaction, and he gave me just the one I was looking for. If he wasn't Uche Agu, he wouldn't have chased me," Lex asserted, wagging a finger. "He would have flipped me off, called me a name and gone on with his life. When he quit Vincenz's pit crew a couple weeks later, that only confirmed it."

Oramus studied the carpet in rumination.

Lex slapped his brother's knee. "Hey, congrats on that race by the way."

A smile broke on Oramus' face, and he grunted. "First and last time I ever beat him."

"There would have been more," Lex assured.

"So why aren't we dead by now?" Oramus asked after a brief intermission.

"Uche and Igwe's deaths were fatal to the syndicate. It's near-extinct now. Amadi lost interest long before we came along, and I think Nwanneka finally realized his mortality. Losing Uche demoralized him. I guess he decided to mourn in peace, before he ended up dead himself. Tears ran rampant for fifteen years before it finally plummeted."

"You don't have any idea what they did with my family, do you?"

Lex sighed. "I wish I had something for you. I heard rumors they did the same thing to another woman several years prior, but details—there are none."

"I guess you know why Igwe kidnapped my wife."

"Papers said he had bets on the race; he couldn't let you win, or he'd lose money." Lex leaned back in his chair, verdant irises sparkling.

"That was the police's official excuse, because they couldn't find evidence to prove their real suspicion."

"Vincenz?"

Oramus half-smiled, cheeks burning; he nodded.

"I thought so. How'd you figure it out?" Lex ventured.

"First, there was a recording from Igwe's answering machine. The voice on the tape hired Igwe to keep me from the race, but they couldn't trace the call. Then I ran into Rudy Vincenz. It was after Gwen was out of the hospital, and we were back home. She was about eight months pregnant then. We were at church on a Sunday morning. It was a big church—the biggest in Austin.

~

Oramus held his wife's hand while gently tapping his leg to an upbeat gospel chorus. People stood all around them, clapping and swaying and singing. Oramus eyed an elderly couple at his side. Gray hair sat upon the woman's head like cotton candy fluff. Her husband, head bald and spotted, bent forward, gripping the pew in front of him. Oramus could barely see the pulpit between people's butts.

"I told Satan," he mumbled in rhythm, "get thee behind. Victory today is mine."

Oramus noticed a man in pin-stripes walking toward the vestibule. Recognition came like a snakebite: Rudy Vincenz. He let go of Gwen's hand, mouthing "I'll be right back."

She nodded, and Oramus wove past the line of churchgoers in his pew. He sped up the aisle, through two wooden doors manned by ushers. Catching the door close on the men's room, Oramus pursued. He waltzed into the restroom, adopting an easy pace. Vincenz stood at a urinal. Oramus ambled to the sinks and leisurely began washing his hands. His quarry took the next basin shortly. Drying his hands on a brown paper towel, Oramus said, "Rudy?"

Vincenz glanced into the mirror at his sinkmate. A flash of dread dashed over his face, swiftly concealed by a yellow grin. "Oramus."

"What are you doing here?"

"Pastor's a friend of mine." He shook his hands of excess water and went for a towel. "You live in Austin?"

"Yeah. My wife and I."

After throwing away the wet towel, Vincenz clasped his old competitor's hand. "How's she doing?"

"Fine."

Rudy's quaking hands dangled briefly before burrowing into their pockets. "Well. Good to see you again."

Oramus threw on a smile. "You too."

~

"He left in the middle of the sermon."

"Did you know it was him right away?"

"No. I knew something was wrong, the way he was acting, but it wasn't until later that night that it clicked. I realized it was his voice—"

"On the recording."

Oramus nodded.

After another short silence, Lex said, "Oramus, remember when Dad used to pray with us?"

"Yeah," Oramus replied hoarsely.

"That was just about all the religion we ever got. And I'm wondering. What are your religious views now?"

Oramus filled his lungs and let the air flow out his lips. "I don't really have any. Not anymore."

"Not anymore." Lex repeated. "Well, what were they?"

"I believed in God."

"But you don't now."

"I don't know, Lex. He just doesn't concern me."

Lex mulled over his brother's answer. "Well, I'm concerned. You know, I hope hell isn't how they describe it to you in the Bible. The lake of fire and all that; burning alive for all eternity. I've done a lot of bad things, but I don't think I quite deserve that. Hell should be something more like a coma. You know, you just go to sleep one night and never wake up. It makes more sense when you think about it—for a God of mercy. I don't think punishment is what people need in the afterlife. They need peace. And heaven's just a bonus," Lex chuckled. "Either you go to heaven and live in perfect happiness forever, or you go nowhere and never have to think or worry ever again. In fact, I'm not sure I'd want to live for eternity at all. Even if it is in heaven. I think going to sleep knowing my consciousness will never return may be the most comforting feeling I can imagine. If God is as merciful as the Good Book says he is, maybe he'll grant me that."

~

Fitch burst into the apartment, abandoning the doorknob to punch the wall like a battering ram. Muttering profanity, he threw his backpack on the floor and began loosening his belt. After struggling to remove a pair of jeans over his tennis shoes, he reached for a pair of sweatpants lying on the couch and stepped into them. Finally, stripped down to a muscle-shirt, Fitch sprinted out the open door, slamming it in his wake.

The joss house had two levels. The top level was smaller than the bottom like a wedding cake in a shell of pea-green slats and jalapeño shingles. Fitch ran up the small, concrete lot, a dark spike of sweat pointing down his chest. He jogged through the empty doorframe and fluidly launched into a bout of push-ups. Sweat dripped from his nose into a tiny pool on the ground. He smelled the green tea and incense already.

"I suppose I don't have to tell you you're late," said an aged voice. "Again." Two clean, bare feet walked into Fitch's field of vision. Above a set of well-groomed toenails, Fitch could see the bottoms of his mentor's maroon training pants.

"Remind me what time you get out of class today." The voice dripped condescension.

Dipping and pressing interminably, Fitch answered, "Four."

"How long would you say is your commute from the university?"

"Fifteen-minute walk. Eight-minute run."

"So according to your estimates, you should arrive here by four-ten, four-fifteen. What is the time right now?"

"Four-thirty."

"Four-forty. Care to explain why this is the third time you've been tardy this month?"

"I had to go back to the apartment for my clothes."

"And what else?"

Fitch paused. "My professor—"

"Don't lie, Fitch. It's impolite. You're digging yourself into a hole. If I offer you a shovel, it's to pull you out, not for you to dig faster."

Fitch's push-ups slowed. "Class let out early, so I went to the library."

"Looking for?"

"I was searching the database for issues of the *Detroit Free Press,* and I lost track of time."

"You were looking for articles about your father, no doubt? You can stand up now."

Fitch collapsed onto one knee. After a moment of rest, he climbed to his feet with a great sigh, standing almost half-a-foot taller than his mentor. The scrawny man wore a handmade training outfit of thin pants and a shirt tied at the waist. Far below the summit of his clean-shaven scalp, two white tributaries flowed from his upper lip into a reservoir on his chin. He stood, unwavering as a lighthouse.

"Only for purposes of Parcere," said Fitch. His chest continually swelled and deflated.

A hint of cheerfulness washed over the mentor's face. He turned into the south wing of the joss house, Fitch close behind. The joss house had an east-west breezeway with two rooms on the bottom floor and one on top. Stairways to the top room were located in each of the wings. The house was a public venue, situated between a street and a garden. All doorframes were bare, and rooms vacant.

In the south wing, the mentor had set up a portable stove of four stick legs, a small coal-chamber and a clay plate. The contraption currently warmed a painted teakettle.

Two nested cups sat on the ground. Fitch picked them up. His mentor took the kettle and began pouring. "Let's walk."

The pair meandered west, into the garden. They strode out onto a wide, enclosed boulevard lined with evergreens, over which rose stalks of the Hanoi skyline. A few Hanoiians sat on benches, strolled or walked pets through the garden behind the evergreen barrier. A labyrinth of tiny paths wandered through the greenery, all emptying into the main strip. Fitch recognized several frequenters. A heavyset man of middle-age was peeling a tangerine closeby. He waved to Fitch and his mentor every day like an eager child waving to his favorite animal in the zoo.

They veered down a side-path. Through the evergreens lay a grove of plantlife only a botanist could discern. Fitch marveled at the colors: soft pinks and lavenders interspersed with deep rusts and indigoes, all encased in plentiful, supernatural green. Fitch inhaled the sanctuary, as if to hoard the scent for his nostrils alone.

"I'm glad you're beginning to see Parcere on the horizon," said Fao-cun softly to match the quiet of the garden. Even traffic noises found difficulty filtering through the vegetation. "And I think you'll miss school next week."

Fitch smiled.

"I'll book your plane ticket tonight."

"Where?"

"Austin. Telephone me after it's finished, and I'll feed you the location of your mother."

"My mother?" Fitch shot in disbelief.

146

The mentor rooted himself before his pupil. "You dispute me." He spat the words like saltwater.

For the first time in a long while, Fitch feared his mentor.

"Your father's name wasn't the only one you searched at the library, was it? What was the other name?"

Fitch choked.

"*What was the other name?*"

"Gwendolen Alby."

"Ah ha," sighed the mentor, faking epiphany.

"I don't understand why—"

"Because she's a distraction!" he roared. "You must remain focused. Trim the fat."

Fitch gazed above to the nigh impregnable canopy.

"Look at me," the mentor demanded. "Your mother was a vessel, through which your father could give you life. That's it. She is nothing more. Sacrifice is a must in all religions. Ours is no different."

Fitch nodded compliantly. "How?"

The mentor resumed their stroll. "The inland taipan is the most venomous snake in existence. Just one bite is toxic enough to kill one hundred adult humans. Taipans are only found in central Australia, and I have a herpetologist contact in Mackay who can get ahold of some for me. You'll have two vials of the venom and one of the anti-venom. I want you to inject yourself with the anti-venom. Do you understand me?"

"Why?"

"For several reasons. Most importantly, for your own safety. You should take all precautions necessary in case something goes awry. Also, it's healthy to know first-hand what you're inflicting on another individual. The anti-venom won't be pleasant. It's a sign of good faith and commitment to your cause. And have no doubt that I will test your blood when you return."

"Why not do it before I leave, so you can see?"

"No; I want you to do it on your own, when I'm not watching."

Questions began rising like helium balloons. "How does the venom work?" Fitch asked.

"First, vomiting. Then muscular paralysis kicks in, followed by respiratory failure. Pain will be brief. They'll be dead in under forty-five minutes."

"Why venom?"

"It's simple; it works fast; difficult to trace; and it's a formidable death. Guns are petty," he censured.

"Fao-cun," Fitch began timidly. "Can I ask you a personal question?"

"Ask whatever you like."

"How did you liberate your father?"

The mentor didn't respond immediately. "My father died before I was born," he said. "Tuberculosis took him."

Fitch sensed his questioning was over.

"Listen," the mentor ordered. "Wear gloves. Make sure all your skin is covered, so they can't scratch you. Avoid carpets if you can. If not, remember to erase your footprints with an unused, soft-bristle brush. Just be smart, and you should be all right." He laid a hand on Fitch's shoulder. "Chúc may mắn."

"Cám ơn ông."

~

Oramus stood at the doorstep of his motel room.

"See you tomorrow," said Lex, trekking down the row of numbered doors, when he unwittingly bumped into a young man of fighter build going the opposite direction. "Sorry."

Oramus quietly slipped back into his room. His re-latching the chain was halted by a knock at the door; he cracked it. The young man Lex bumped stood outside, wearing a black windbreaker, sweats and a backpack. His hair was blonde and prickly and his hands were concealed in-pocket.

"Can I help you?" asked Oramus.

"Are you in the blue car?"

"Yeah."

"I think somebody smashed your windshield."

Oramus sighed, suddenly feeling the effects of the hour. "Thanks."

"I'm Drake." He pulled a mittened hand out of the windbreaker and offered to shake.

Oramus conceded, meeting the firmest grip he had ever encountered.

~

Oramus awoke to a faint, icy splash on his cheek. He cracked his eyes, letting a yellow gleam sear his eyeballs. All was hazy. A large, black figure hovered over him. Oramus blinked, scrambling for orientation. His memory soon flooded back with his focus. Throat raw, he detected a familiar flavor on his tongue. Oramus had thrown up. He could smell it now, too, and his chest felt wet. The man above him in the black windbreaker straightened up and disappeared. Oramus released a groan intended to form words as he attempted rolling onto one side. His body didn't budge. He concentrated on raising a finger. Fruitless still. The figure returned momentarily, holding a tape recorder in blue latex hands.

"You've been out for half an hour. Fao-cun wanted you to hear this," he said. Oramus watched him set the object down on the bed and heard the click of a button, followed by breath in a microphone. The man backed up to a wall and crouched down out of sight.

"Hello, Oramus. Have a look at yourself. Racing didn't turn out very well for you, did it? I warned you it wouldn't. This creature you've become is your doing. I had plans for you, but you rejected them. So I let you go and started from scratch. And eventually, I got where I wanted to be. What about you, Oramus? I don't know if it means anything now, but I did miss you. I may have been frustrated, but I wanted to see you."

Oramus felt a strong tingling in his nose, and sobs crept up like bandits.

"There's something I never told you. It seems irrelevant now, but it's always bothered me. I told that thug in Detroit where you lived. He'd threatened my life; what else could I do?" He paused. "I don't think you deserve what happened to you, but you could have prevented it. At least I've given you the opportunity to go out with some dignity. That is my last gift to you. I wish you had made better choices, Oramus." The breathing continued for just a second more, and the machine cut off.

Windbreaker retrieved the device and began making his exit.

Oramus forced a murmur, barely able to form syllables. "You look just like her."

The door shut.

~

The plain was dead. A cyst on the planet's face. While water is the life-potion, down here it was vicious like an exiled sub-breed. Fitch zoomed across the ice on a snowmobile with another in tow. His featureless surroundings gave the illusion that he wasn't moving at all. The guys at the base some miles back asked too many questions. He landed on the airstrip about six hours ago, and they hadn't ceased grilling him since. Visitors were no doubt rare. Their questions were likely founded as much in boredom as suspicion. After he arrived, Fitch had to wait around for a meal. He suspected that the men purposely postponed the meal in order to prolong their interrogation over too many games of rummy. When Fitch finally got away, he chained two snowmobiles together and borrowed the station's GPS. His mentor had sent his mother's coordinates via e-mail.

The prison was twenty-six miles out of the station. Fitch had traveled a little more than twenty-five. It was the longest fifty minutes of his life. He stopped the snowmobile and glassed the area. He scanned for nearly a minute before finding anything that resembled an entry. He glided over to the landmark. As he got closer, the thing looked more and more like a formation of ice. Fitch dismounted and returned to his binoculars. This time, he found the entrance almost instantly. He was sure. The glacial deformity was unmistakably unnatural: a rigid trapezoid jutting from the ice like a sunken ship. He sailed up to the little shell. Standing at a trap door on one incline of the trapezoid, he removed a pistol from his parka. Caution didn't matter here.

Fitch tapped the door with the head of his pistol. Several seconds later, a loud screech announced its opening.

"Who's there?"

Fitch kicked the door agape and shot. At his feet, two rosy cheeks drained of color. A pair of blue eyes as round as quarters stared up at him from under a soft, gray bowl-cut. The man's fingers slackened on the handrail as blood spurted from his collar. Gradually, he sunk backward into a roll down the steep set of steps, crashing at the bottom like a sandbag. Fitch followed him down and unclipped a set of keys from the warden's belt.

Of the ten cells, only three were occupied. The closest on the left detained a lean, young man standing in a corner. Further down, a feral being clung to his cell door like an ape.

"You fuck!" he screamed. "You shot him, you fuck!" As the inmate howled, his bloodshot eyes pierced through a nest of matted hair.

Fitch looked to the third cell, last on the right. His mother sat inside, pale, thin and grimy. She watched him, unafraid but not bold. Fitch strode toward her, clacking down the catwalk. Suddenly, a claw sprang from the wild man's cage. Fitch weaved, and the pistol clapped once again.

"Emmerich!" his mother yelped.

The wild man cradled his dripping torso and collapsed. Hands gloved in blood, he laid back his head, blinking like a docile, tranquilized beast and bobbed to sleep.

Fitch remained frozen for a second or two. Thawing, he stuffed the pistol into his coat pocket and began sifting through keys, until one agreed with the lock on his mother's cell. He knelt before the weeping prisoner, unshouldered a backpack and fished out a fruit jar of some cloudy liquor. Stoppering his breath, he unscrewed the lid and calmly gripped her nape. After a few passes of the jar beneath her nostrils, his mother wilted. He lowered her to the ground, unfolding her legs from beneath her. He resacked the jar of homemade knockout gas in exchange for a hard, black case. Inside, three syringes lay side-by-side: one empty, one venom-filled, one of antivenom.

Fitch fixed his gaze on his mother's face. Beneath the layer of grime, he could tell she was fair. She must have been beautiful once. Her lips were now cavernous. Her hair had to be at least a meter in length. He thought she looked royal, like pictures he had seen of serene, Native American queens.

No turning back now. Fitch knew he could never face her. He took out the first syringe and went to work.

~

The mentor waited at the joss house with a glass of ice water. It was a hot day. The glass sweated like an athlete. An occasional draft through the breezeway pressed the shirt against his lower back, cool and damp. He spread his fingers to feel the wind rush between them. Rising to the balls of his feet, he began a solitary waltz to no music. Like a drunken marionette, he twirled around the joss house, arms outstretched, wrists limp.

As Fitch approached from the street in his habitual attire, the mentor's dance grew rusty and defunct. He extended an arm, drawing Fitch into a hug.

"You're feeling jovial," said Fitch.

"Parcere is a holiday!" the mentor admitted. "There's water in the next room. You must be parched."

"I could use something wet."

The mentor led Fitch into the south wing. "I also have a brisket warming here on the stove. Not that it would need the stove to keep warm." A wicker table and two chairs sat in the middle of the room.

"Thanks for the homecoming."

"It's nothing. Sit."

Fitch did as instructed. The mentor picked up a large, covered dish at the stove and carried it to the table. "Give me your arm," he bade, pulling a small apparatus from his pocket.

Again, Fitch obeyed innately.

The mentor clamped his palm like pliers. "Keep your index finger stiff. This works very similar to a diabetic's glucose meter." He touched the machine to Fitch's fingertip. There was quick sting. "It takes a sample of your blood and tests for neurotoxins." A narrow slip of paper soaked up the blood-bead decorating Fitch's finger and retracted like a tongue. "Now let's give it a minute to process." He put the meter on the table and peeled foil from the dish, where a pile of blackish brown meat awaited. "Eat up!"

The mentor sat down, and they dug in, seizing the stringy lumps with their fingers.

The meter beeped. The old man observed its results. "It's positive."

"Fao-cun," Fitch asked, cheeks bulging, "our relationship is different now, right? I'm no longer your pupil."

"Well, technically yes, but I can't promise I'll never teach you anything again. I'm hardwired for it."

"Of course," he conceded, stuffing in another strip. "But we can speak as equals now, yes?"

"If you wish."

Fitch swallowed. "Then tell me something. Your father died when you were young. So did your mother raise you?"

Fao-cun licked his fingers, wiped them on his shirt and laced them under his chin. He had barely eaten. "Yes, my mother had a hand in my rearing."

Fitch grunted and shoveled in another slice of meat. "Did you kill her?"

Fao-cun exhaled. "No. She died an old crone in Laos." He scratched the bridge of his nose while Fitch chewed a mouthful. His eyes narrowed. "Fitch, are you unhappy with me? And my orders?"

"I have a question concerning you and my father."

"What weren't you able to gather from the tape and the library?"

"Just one thing." Fitch blasted to his feet, striding for the stove. He had managed to barrel through a third of the dish. "When that thug shook you down in Detroit, you sent him to the hotel hoping he would kill my grandfather, didn't you?"

"That man wasn't your grandfather," Fao-cun spat.

"Tell me I'm wrong. You're an opportunist. You wanted it to happen, so you could have my father for yourself." Fitch laughed in disbelief. "You killed a man for his son. Twice." He felt hollow as a cadaver.

Fao-cun stood calmly. "All you need to know is that I loved your father. Like a son." He walked monk-like to Fitch, reaching for the boy's shoulder. "The way I love you."

In a flash, Fitch snatched two legs of the portable stove and swung it like a baseball bat, hammering through the elder's kneecaps. Fao-cun pounded the concrete face-first onto a few glowing coals as Fitch let the stove crash into the opposite wall with a long, reverberating clang.

The rage left Fitch short-winded and staggering. Nausea surged through him, and a mound of soggy, slimy brisket clapped the floor near Fao-cun's bloody face. Fao-cun pathetically spit out a tooth cocooned in blood and looked up at his former student, who was rummaging through his backpack. He removed the last of the three syringes. It was half-full.

"I saved some for you." Fitch knelt by the crippled man's side and yanked the arm from under his chest. "A half-dose should be just as lethal." He plunged the needle carelessly into the flaccid limb.

"Fitch," the old man gurgled. "Fitch."

"What?"

"This moment—this is your Parcere."

Fitch emptied the syringe. "I've already killed my father."

Fao-cun hacked violently in response, garnishing the floor with specks of blood.

Fitch fell from haunches to back, abandoning the syringe in Fao-cun's arm. He turned his head and vomited again.

~

Fitch pricked his mother's arm and depressed the pump. The yellow taipan antidote flushed into her veins and was gone. His decision was sealed. Fitch ensured he could not change his mind. He refused to confront her a murderer. And there was only one guarantee.

~

Fitch rolled over and tried to push himself up. He wedged one knee under him, then the other. Slowly, he attempted to stand, shaking like a newborn fawn, and lunged for the doorframe. From where he leaned, he had a clear view of the empty street to the east. Fitch looked at the ground and blinked hard repeatedly. His vision was fading. Before he could take another step, the floor rose up and smacked his face.

~

"911. What is your location?"

"Mo'Rest Motel."

"Please state the emergency."

"I think my brother's dead."

"An ambulance is on its way."

~

Lex walked through the automatic glass doors, eyes set on the gray Grand Cherokee waiting on the other side. Beyond the dry portico, clean, Rocky Mountain snow padded the landscape. The driver-door of the Cherokee slammed, and an elated woman in her thirties came peeling around the front of the car. Lex threw the black duffel bag from his shoulder and caught her. The collision almost tackled him. After setting her back down on the dark red brick, his hands moved up to her shoulders.

"How'd it go, babe?" she asked. "You sounded upset on the phone."

"Well, I got to talk to him." Lex opened the back door and tossed his luggage on the seat. "Not as much as I'd have liked to."

"Why? What happened?"

"Well, we were supposed to meet for lunch, but he didn't show. So I went back to his motel room and found him—dead."

"Oh my god! Was he sick?" she demanded, brown eyes imploring.

"I don't think so."

"Then what?"

Lex stopped her speaking with a kiss on her copper forehead. He bathed a hand in her soft, black tresses. "Let's just go home."

Epilogue

Gwen awoke nauseous. She smelled puke. The bitter stench was almost suffocating. Once her eyes focused, she saw a thin pool near her face reminiscent of chocolate milk. Lying on her side away from the others, Gwen wondered how she got there. She wrung out her memory, and it was hardly seconds before she remembered the intruder. Why had he come? What did he do? Suddenly, her mind relaxed; he was a dream.

Gwen rolled over to see if anyone else was awake. Emmerich was sprawled on the floor, still sleeping. How early was it? Gwen stared at the ceiling, rubbing the scar on her abdomen. She could still see the face from last night. It was as vivid as if he was on the ceiling staring back at her. Normally she couldn't remember the faces of people from her dreams, like featureless smudges on a painting. But the intruder was different. She could sculpt his face in detail. There was something familiar about it.

Gwen sat up and examined her gray pullover the company sent a few months ago. Only a little vomit had gotten on the sleeve. She surveyed the rest of the jail. The new Australian, Gervais, slept upright, holding his knees in a corner of the cell. A different pilot brought him; an Asian. They had taken Dolores long ago.

Something made Gwen jump. She saw Ambrose lying like a dropped toy at the foot of the stairs. She rose and covered her mouth, afraid of waking someone with a scream. She glanced in Emmerich's cell. The man wasn't asleep. His gut and his arms were dyed red. Gwen knew she had not dreamt. A ring of keys dangled from the lock in her door. She nudged the door with her fingertips. Its spectral groan accentuated the prison's tomblike silence. Recovering the key-ring, Gwen stumbled down the catwalk to unlock the Aussie's door. Then, reluctantly bypassing Ambrose' corpse, she clambered up the stairs to the overhead door and closed her fingers around a lever. It felt like squeezing an icicle. The lever released the door, which took some force to open. Immediately, her face began to ache in the airstream. She let the door fall, crawling out into the snow. The subzero winds cut through her attire. She could have been wearing nothing at all. Gwen rose, stupefied, to her feet. The snow wet her socks. Yards from where she stood, a snowmobile was parked. Gwen slowly approached and swung her leg over the vehicle. A pair of gloves rested on the handlebars. She donned them quickly and turned the key already in the ignition. The vehicle sputtered to life. A GPS screen shimmered between the handlebars. Brushing off some caked snow, she read, *Destination: Airstrip. 26 miles.* An arrow indicated the apt direction. Gwen pressed the accelerator under her foot, and the snowmobile lurched into transit.

Annually over the past twenty years, Gwen would enter a spell in which only those she missed occupied her thoughts. For the first few months of her incarceration, they consisted mainly of her mother, husband and baby. As years passed though, the list expanded. In recent spells, her thoughts reached out to people from her childhood, acquaintances, some people she barely knew at all. There was the bicyclist she passed every morning on her way to class. He wore athletic shorts, a spandex shirt, leather gloves, sunglasses, a helmet, everything. He smiled and waved every morning. Gwen wondered how long he continued taking that route after she was gone. Was he still alive, still biking? There was her English professor, Dr. Mendel, who conducted class in a circle. He spoke in a slow drawl, like syrup flowing off pancakes. One had to cling to every word in order to retain an ounce of meaning. He was timid; he smiled slowly and gestured slowly and often spoke with his hands. He fostered in her a love of Blake and Browning, Dickinson and Bradstreet, O'Connor and Chopin. Had age claimed him?

At the current moment, racing across the dead, white prairie, one of these thoughts paid Gwen a visit, not unwelcome but unexpected. A memory of her first dog slithered in. It was her father's bird-dog, Shep. She didn't really remember much about the dog itself—the girl couldn't have been more than four-years-old. She could only remember the trauma of losing it. Her mother told her Shep had wandered off into the woods. She said the coyotes got him, and that's why he never came back. The news was deafening to the little girl. Now something struck the middle-aged woman that had never crossed her mind before: the oddity that coyotes would make a meal of virtually one of their own. The savagery of it astounded her. Canines eating other canines.